Cat Walker was born and raised in Minnesota, USA, where she first developed her love of creative writing. In 2006, she visited Ireland and fell in love, literally. She moved to Ireland in January 2007, and now lives in County Meath with her Ireland-born husband, and spends her time expanding her imagination and enjoying the beautiful Irish countryside.

To my exceptional twin sister, thank you for always encouraging me to follow my dreams.

Cat Walker

CHANCE BEGINNING

AUSTIN MACAULEY PUBLISHERS™

LONDON * CAMBRIDGE * NEW YORK * SHARJAH

A CIP catalogue record for this title is available from the British Library.

ISBN 9781035868131 (Paperback)
ISBN 9781035868148 (ePub e-book)

www.austinmacauley.com

First Published 2024
Austin Macauley Publishers Ltd®
1 Canada Square
Canary Wharf
London
E14 5AA

Also by Cat Walker

Irish Fireworks

The evidence was irrefutable. He had him. How the police had missed it, Douglas wasn't sure, but that suited him just fine, and with a few minor adjustments, the police would never know.

Glancing at his phone, he saw that it was nearly 5:30. *Perfect*, he smiled. Picking up his phone, he set the plan in motion. By the end of the month, he'd be well on his way to the senate. He chuckled as he moved his mouse over the series of digital photos that would serve as the bait to lure the man in the pictures into seeing things his way; and if that didn't work, there were other ways to get what he wanted.

"Hello?" The man on the other end of the line had an obvious eastern European accent.

Douglas kept the conversation short. "I have another job for you. Meet me in 10 minutes. The usual place."

There was no confirmation, just the sound of the phone being hung up.

Douglas had no doubt the man would meet him. He was a professional and would have suggested another time if it didn't suit.

Glancing at his pc again, he copied the file onto a USB stick, and then as he closed the file, there was a discreet knock on his door. "Come in," was his reply, knowing that it was his legal assistant.

Kiera Davidson peeked her head in the door. "I just need your signature for the Allen settlement."

He motioned her in and as he signed his name where she indicted, he glanced at the USB stick he had just ejected. He'd need to make another copy, he decided, and as his assistant quietly closed the door behind her, he slid a second USB into the USB port and began to copy the images and the letter to the stick.

Reaching in his desk drawer, he grabbed a blank envelope and put the USB stick, and the letter he had printed, inside it.

Smiling, he couldn't help but laugh at the irony of it all. As the district attorney, he had built up many connections; some on the level and others that, if discovered, could mean the end of his career and very possibly prison. But they were also the connections that would get him elected as a senator.

He had been doing some research into the man who currently held the Republican senate seat, and it was that research that was now sitting in front of him. Millstone had held the office far too long, and with the next election only 2 years away, Stephen knew he had to act now. With what he had here, he had no doubt that the senate seat would be his for the taking. Picking up the envelope, he smiled and thought, *now we have him.* Once the good senator got the USB stick, he'd have no choice but to play ball.

*****

Kiera glanced at the clock and saw that it was time to leave for the day, and closing the document she had just printed, she absently moved her mouse over and hit shut down on her PC. It was then that she realized that she hadn't printed off her boarding pass.

"Shit!" She said aloud, failing to check the curse as her boss emerged from his office.

"Such language," he teased.

"Sorry." Kiera couldn't help but blush.

"What's wrong?" He asked as he reached for his overcoat. It was pouring outside and while his meeting was just around the corner, he wasn't willing to get drenched.

"I forgot to print off my boarding pass," Kiera explained as she reached for the on button to restart her pc again.

Stephen quickly considered the options. He didn't want Kiera around when he got back, just in case he needed some privacy, but he wasn't in the habit of letting her use his laptop either. He knew that the document was closed and filed away, and he knew that Kiera hadn't been a snoop before so it should be fine. "Why don't you use my laptop?" he offered.

"Are you sure?" Kiera verified. She had been working for Stephen Douglas as his legal assistant for over three years and he had always made it clear that she was not to use his laptop.

"I know your computer," he replied. "You'll still be here in an hour waiting for it to boot up." And he didn't want that. Besides, he had agreed to her extended vacation because there were a few things he wanted to get done without her being around and he didn't want to risk her missing her flight.

"Thanks boss, it will only take a couple of minutes."

"No problem; just shut it down before you leave." Then as he headed out the door, he called back, "Have a good vacation, I'll see you in a couple of weeks."

Kiera waved goodbye as he left the office and then grabbing the USB stick she had copied her documents onto, she slipped into his office to print off her boarding pass.

*****

She had made a mistake. A huge mistake.

Kiera had plugged in her memory key into Stephen's laptop to print the copy of her itinerary and boarding pass, and after successfully sending the documents to print, she had ejected the USB and had set it down on the desk while she reached under his desk to grab her copies. Why he had installed the printer under his desk had always been strange to her, but he said that despite the inconvenience, it saved him time. Retrieving her USB stick, she had shut down his laptop and headed home.

It wasn't until she had gotten home that she had discovered her mistake. She planned to take her USB stick with her on her vacation in case she needed to print any off anything again, and she had slid it into her personal computer to double-check that she had a copy of her passport on the stick. It was then that she had discovered her mistake. As soon as she opened the USB drive, she had seen that she had inadvertently grabbed the wrong memory stick.

The contents of the stick were instantly visible on her screen, and as she scrolled her mouse over the preview images, it shocked her. The photos were explicit and graphic, and the letter she found was obviously blackmail. Kiera knew that she had stumbled on something very dangerous.

She reread the letter, confident that she had misread the letters intent, but she hadn't, and then she quickly downloaded everything onto her laptop and then onto another memory key.

As she copied the contents, she realized that she would also need to copy her travel details onto another USB stick, and then the full realization of what she had done hit her. As soon as Stephen looked at the USB stick that was still on his desk, he would realize what she had done, and then she feared that she would be in real trouble.

Since she had worked for Stephen, she had never once doubted his integrity; until now. What she had found had shocked and scared her and she knew, beyond a shadow of a doubt, that once he found out what she knew, that her life would be in danger.

Looking down at the copy of the USB stick, she wondered briefly why she had made a second copy of the stick; protection, she supposed. Once he discovered that she had seen the files, then having a copy may give her some sort of leverage. But more importantly, she knew that he'd have to be stopped.

Damn it, all she had wanted to do was to print off her boarding pass and get on with her vacation…instead, she had landed herself in a heap of trouble.

Perfect! she thought. *Now what am I going to do?* she asked herself.

She was due to leave on a two-week holiday to Mexico, but now she wondered if it would be a wise choice. She had no way of knowing when Stephen would look at the USB stick again, and even if he realized that she had taken the key, there was no way for him to know that she had seen what was on the key. After all, she had printed off her boarding pass as she had said she would, and for all practical purposes, she shouldn't have had to even look at the key again until she returned from her trip. Perhaps she was worried needlessly. However, if she contacted the police about the files now, he'd know that she had turned him in and then she'd be in real danger. The contents of the USB convinced her of that. On the other hand, maybe she could wait, and send the file anonymously while she was on her vacation. Maybe then, he wouldn't get suspicious, and by the time she returned from her trip, she would have her game face on and maybe she could pretend that she hadn't seen anything.

No, it was no good, she decided. As soon as Stephen discovered the mix-up, he would come after her, and… she shuddered at the possible consequences that sprung to mind.

Glancing around her bedroom, she realized that she still had to finish packing for her trip and there were a few things she had wanted to get done before she was due to fly out later that evening. That was, if she even went on the trip. Burying her head in her hands, she wondered what she should do.

*****

The officer looked up from the report he had been working on to see the desk sergeant heading his way with a young lady in tow. From the look of her, she looked frightened and he quickly saved the document and focused his attention on the woman.

Kiera was ushered into a room and given some water. She began to tell the kind man that she thought she was in danger, and then began to outline what had happened.

She had decided that her safest move was to go directly to the police and that her trip would have to wait. She had travel insurance after all, and she was sure that escaping a criminal would fall under the category of an emergency.

She had been at the police station for over an hour and she was tired. Grabbing her backpack, she stepped out of the interrogation room, and she headed for the coffee room. The officer had taken her there when she had first arrived, and she decided that another cup of the horrible stuff couldn't hurt. Where it lacked in taste, it more than made up for in strength. As she left the interrogation room, Kiera stopped when she saw a man whom she recognized. Ducking into the coffee room, she felt sure that she had seen him before he had seen her, at least she hoped she had. What was he doing here?

Was she being paranoid or was that one of Stephan's informants? Hazarding another glance, she caught sight of him as he was talking to one of the police officers. She studied his face and knew that she was right. It was a face that was not easy to forget. She had seen Stephen with him on a couple of occasions and she had always had an uneasy feeling about him. While he was quite handsome, he had a dark menacing look about him and she had always wondered what Stephen was doing with such a dangerous looking character.

Somehow, she didn't believe that it was a coincidence that he was at the police station, and if it was, she certainly couldn't let him see her. She was supposed be on a flight to Mexico, and if he told Stephen, then he would know for sure that she had found the files; and if her instincts and the sick feeling she had in her stomach were right, then she was in danger even here.

Sneaking out of the coffee room, she headed toward the elevator, catching it just before the doors were closing. She glanced back again as the elevator door was closing, but this time they locked eyes, and the look in his eyes told her that she needed to move. Fast.

As soon as the elevator door opened, she slung her backpack onto her back, and she ran. Thoughts of her vacation vanished, as she realized that she needed to find a safe place to hide.

Slowing to catch her breath, she saw a bus approaching the next stop and she picked up speed, making it to the stop in time to step onto the bus before the driver closed the doors.

Making her way to an open seat, Kiera reached into her pocket and pulled out her phone. Scrolling down her list of contacts, she dialed the one person she knew could help her.

One Month Later
Chicago

Sari couldn't believe her luck. The falcons were very active, and the moonlight was perfect.

An amateur wildlife photographer, Sari had decided to work late at her job as a network specialist to take advantage of the full moon, and the promised forecast of a clear sky. She had already gotten several photos of the birds in flight, and she was pleased with the results.

Zooming in on two birds as they perch on the building across the way, Sari saw a movement to her left. Turning, she focused in on the top of the adjacent building.

She caught the movement again and watched as she saw two men fighting. Without thinking, she began to take pictures as she watched the huskier of the two men, push the other man away. When she saw a flash of light, she realized in horror that he had shot him. Two more flashes of light told her that he had shot him again. Then she watched as he walked over to the man, now lying on the rooftop and then he fired a fourth time. Shaking, Sari reached for the phone next to her and dialed 911.

"Emergency Services, how can I help you?"

"I just saw a man shoot another man on the rooftop of the US Bank building."

"On the rooftop?"

"Yes!"

"How did you witness this? Are you on the rooftop as well?"

"No, I'm in the office building across the street. Please hurry." Looking up, she gasped, "Oh my god." Sari put the phone down and backed away from the window as she saw the gunman looking in her direction. He couldn't possibly see her, right? The room was dark. Focusing the lens again, she saw that he had received a phone call and was now looking in her direction. Turning, she ran for the elevator. But she stopped herself before she hit the down button. What if he knew that she had seen him, or if someone had tipped him off that she was there? Oh god. What was she going to do? If she went downstairs now, she'd be an easy target.

"Think!" she said aloud.

He couldn't have seen her, she reasoned. From the outside, the windows were like mirrors, and without any lights on, he couldn't have seen her. Could he? She didn't think so, but he was looking right at her.

Turning toward the stairs, she ran down three flights to the 52nd floor. Running down the hall to the storage room, she opened the door and turned on the light. She could hang out here until morning. But before she could do that, she knew that there was one more thing she had to do.

Turning around, she ran into the computer room and logged onto the web server. Opening her Google account, she quickly downloaded the photos she had taken and then she emailed them to the Chicago police department, with a note detailing what she had seen and what had happened. Satisfied that was all she could do, she logged off and went back to the storage room where she locked herself in. Turning off the lights, she sat behind some computer boxes, confident that she would be out of sight if someone looked in the room. Then she waited.

*****

Detectives Jason Kollar and Shep Wilson stood studying the scene.

"It looks like a professional hit alright." Shep nodded toward the body. "And considering the vic, it was probably a contracted job."

Jason nodded and looked over at the Wells Fargo Center. Someone had called in the crime but she had been cut off before she could give any more information. He was waiting to hear if her body had been found. The Emergency Services tech had said that the last words out of the woman's mouth had been "Oh my god!"

It did not look good.

"Kollar!" Jason turned and saw Chief John Harrison walking toward him.

"It seems that our witness sent an email to the general information address at the station. Looks like she got some photos sent off after she made her phone call. Unfortunately, the name on the mail account is pretty generic. We're trying to trace it now."

Jason's cell phone rang, it was the Sargent from the team he had sent to search the Wells Fargo Building. "Nothing here, sir. We found the phone she made the call from; it was sitting on the desk. But there's no sign of the woman. If the guy got her, he did her somewhere else. We're dusting for prints now; hopefully, we can ID her."

"Good. I want to know her name as soon as you get it." Hanging up, Jason shook his head and relayed the information to his chief.

*****

Glancing at her watch, Sari saw that it was nearly 6:30 am. It had been about five hours since the murder, so she figured that it would be safe again for her to leave.

She didn't know why, but something told her that going home right now would not be a wise move, so she headed for the police station.

Once there, she asked to see the officer in charge of the US Bank murder case. When asked her name, she said that she would rather wait and tell the person in charge.

Ushered into an office, Sari sat down and waited for someone to join her. She felt a little silly for being so secretive, but the events over the last few hours had left her feeling very cautious. There was something about what she had seen that wasn't 'right'. Not that anything about witnessing a man being murdered was 'right', but there was something that was nagging at her memory and she couldn't quite put her finger on it. Something about what she had seen had her feeling very nervous about her well-being. Probably the fact that the man had seemed to know she had seen it all happen, but she felt sure it was something more.

When the door finally opened, she jumped up and clutched her bag to her chest.

The desk sergeant was right; the woman certainly was edgy, Jason thought as he entered his office. "I'm sorry that I startled you," he said smoothly, trying to calm her. "I'm Detective Jason Kollar." He extended his hand toward her. Taking a deep breath, she unclenched her hand and shook his hand. Closing the door behind him, he motioned toward the chair she had just vacated. "Please have a seat, Miss...?"

17

Sari studied him a moment. He looked trustworthy. He seemed to be waiting for something. Then she realized that he was trying to find out her name.

"I'm sorry," she said, shaking her head. "I'm Sari. Sari Manning."

Kollar blinking in surprise. "Miss Manning?" He had just gotten the results of the fingerprints they had found at the office where the call to Emergency Services had been made from, and they had been in luck. The prints belonged to a Miss Sari Manning who was a registered notary. "We've been looking for you."

Sari frowned. "You have? Why?"

"Well, unless we are mistaken, you were a witness to a crime last night?"

Sari slowly nodded her head. Closing her eyes, she whispered, "Oh god."

Kollar took her by the elbow and lowered her into the chair. He studied her for a moment. There was something about her that seemed familiar, but he couldn't put his finger on it. "Ms. Manning, can you tell me where you were last night?" he asked as he leaned back against his desk.

Nodding again, she took a deep breath. "I sent you an email."

"Yes, we got that, thank you. However, where did you go after you made the call? Did something happen to you?"

"He seemed to know I was there," she whispered. Shaking her head, she knew she wasn't making much sense. "I was calling 911 and I looked back out toward the US Bank building and I saw him looking in my direction. It scared me. I looked back through my lens—"

"Your lens?" he interrupted.

"My camera. I had been taking pictures of the falcons. That's why I was there so late. I was using a zoom lens, that's how I could see everything," she swallowed back the bile she felt rising in her throat, "that's how I could take the pictures." She shuddered again.

"Then what happened?"

"I saw that he was talking on a cell phone and he was looking at me, or at least in my direction. I took off. I ran to the elevator. But…"

She looked down at her hands briefly and noticed for the first time how badly she was shaking. Taking a deep breath, she looked up at him. "I was afraid that he had somehow seen me and knew I was there. It sounds so paranoid now, but I was afraid that since it was so late, that as soon as I walked out of the building, he would know that I had seen him and I would be an easy target."

Kollar nodded his head. "That was a smart assumption."

"I don't know. But I was too chicken to test the theory so I sent the email and then I hid in the storage room."

"Well, that would explain why my men couldn't find you."

"Sorry."

Looking down, she tried to remember if there was anything else, she should tell him. Frowning, she said, "I think that's about it." Then she shook her head again. "No, it isn't. I have a feeling that I saw something else last night that I should remember but can't. I don't know if I can explain it, but something is," she paused, "off," she said awkwardly.

"What do you mean?"

"I'm not sure. I feel like there is a memory just out of reach. Kind of like when you can't remember the name of a song or something. You know what it is, but you can't reach it." Shaking her head again, "I don't know, maybe I'm just imagining it."

"You did have a shocking experience," he tried to sooth her.

"You can say that again." Rubbing her hands over her face, she looked back up at him. "So, what happens now?"

Standing up, Kollar offered her his hand to help her stand. "Now, we get a full statement from you, and I'd like you to sit with a sketch artist as well. I know that you got some pretty incriminating photos of everything, but unfortunately, the face of the murderer was obscured in the images. I'm hoping you will remember something that the camera missed, and our sketch artist is pretty good at pulling out a memory that witnesses can't remember."

Sari nodded and stood up. As he reached for the door, she knew she had to ask him one question. "Before we go out 'there'," she nodded toward the door, "can I ask you a question?"

Kollar nodded and turned his attention toward her.

"The man who was shot, he looked familiar."

Kollar nodded. "Senator Millstone."

"How could…?" Sari took a step back as the gravity of the situation hit her. "Oh god."

He put his hand on her shoulder. "We are going to do everything we can to keep you safe, Ms. Manning."

"The pictures are enough to convict, right?"

Kollar couldn't mislead her. "We will need your testimony as well."

Sari closed her eyes. "Damn! Well, this is another fine mess I've gotten myself into." Kollar couldn't help but smile at her choice of words. Sari looked up at him and saw his smile. "Well, at least I still have my sense of humor."

He studied her for a moment before saying, "Does that mean we can count on your testimony?"

"Of course. I may be a chicken, but I don't usually back down from what is right."

Shaking his head, he smiled at her. "Lady, I wouldn't call you a chicken. Smart, daring. Brave actually. A lot of people would been too afraid to get involved and would have turned a blind eye to what you saw."

Sari just shook her head. "I couldn't do that."

She wondered for a moment if she should say more, but decided it would be best to let it be. *This had nothing to do with… well, it couldn't,* she told herself.

Turning toward the door, she allowed him to escort her from the room.

Over an hour later, Sari had made her statement and had sat with the police sketch artist. Kollar had collected her again and had sat her down in an audiovisual room with his partner, Detective Shep Wilson, and his boss, Chief Harrison.

After a brief introduction, Chief Harrison addressed her, "Miss Manning, I'm sorry to have to ask you to do this, but we'd like to play back the photos you took to verify that nothing is missing."

Sari nodded apprehensively. As the lights were dimmed and the photos began to flash before her, she couldn't help the shudder of fear that once again covered her. It was like watching it all over again. Kollar put a comforting hand on her shoulder and she welcomed it.

She hadn't noticed it at the time, but the gunman's back had been toward her when she had taken the photos, and it hadn't been until after she had taken the last photo that he had turned around. That would explain why they had needed her to sit with the composite artist. She was the only one who had seen the face of the man who had killed the senator.

The last photo showed the man bending over the body of the senator. "Stop," she said suddenly. "There!" she pointed. "What is he doing?"

Kollar stepped forward and took over the controls. Zooming in on the gunman's hand, they saw that he was removing something from the senator's pocket. "Can you isolate that?" he asked the technician.

"Yes sir," was the response.

"It looks like we may have a motive, after all," the technician said as he stared at the picture before him. The gunman had removed an envelope from the dead man's pocket and on it, a name could clearly be read.

"Douglas." Detective Wilson nodded. "Son of a bitch."

Sara couldn't help the shudder that went down her spine. Again, she wondered if she should say more, as she was ushered once again back into Jason's office. Turning toward the detective, Sara was about to tell them her fears when Chief Harrison turned to her. "Ms. Manning, I'd like to thank you for all the help you've provided. I don't think we will need anything else from you today. We have your address, and we'll be in contact should there be anything else we need from you."

"Chief, considering the circumstances, perhaps it would be best if Ms. Manning…" Kollar left the obvious hang in the air.

The chief nodded. "Perhaps you are right. Ms. Manning, is there someplace that you can stay for the next few days?"

Sari felt like she had been punched in the gut. So much for police protection; glancing over at the detective who had been helping her, she saw the shock on his face as well. Looking down, she considered her options. Damn them! She thought. "I'll have to give that some thought," she replied.

Chief Harrison nodded, "Why don't we give you a few minutes? Detectives, I'd like a word with you."

Something didn't feel right about the chief's comment and she suddenly felt very unsafe. As the door closed behind the officers, a thought came to her. Could she just leave? They didn't have any reason to hold her, but she felt nervous that if she called notice to herself, she would be putting herself at more risk. She wondered if perhaps she could sneak out of the station unnoticed, then no one would know where she had gone, and then she could run and hide somewhere. Obviously, the police weren't going to provide her with a place to stay, and if they couldn't guarantee her safety, she might as well try to hide on her own, where no one would be able to find her.

Grabbing the baseball cap and the large sweatshirt she saw hanging on the back of the detective's door, she stuffed them into her bag. Then she walked around the desk and drafted a quick note to the detective and taped it to the back of the door where the items had hung.

Taking a deep breath and saying a quick prayer that this would work, she opened the door and found the men standing nearby. "I just need to use the ladies' room," she said, and when Detective Kollar started to direct her, she said, "I know where it is." Then she turned back toward him, adding, "Thank you."

Walking into the ladies' room, Sari stepped into a stall. No one was in the restroom when she had entered and she thought that had to be a good sign.

Quickly pulling her bag over her head, she pulled the sweatshirt on and zipped it up to her neck and pulled the drawstrings, cinching the hood close to her neck. Then, piling her hair up on the top of her head, she pulled on the baseball cap.

Walking out of the stall, she looked in the mirror and tried to decide if she could get away with it. Then she studied her image again. She wasn't convinced that she would fool anyone. Rooting in the bottom of her bag, she found her sunglasses and put them on her face. Now she thought that she looked a little different; hopefully different enough to get out the door and not be recognized by anyone who knew her.

Saying another quick prayer, she slipped out of the room and headed for the elevator.

*****

She couldn't believe she had actually made it without being caught. She had made it to the elevator without being stopped, but she knew she had to hurry. They wouldn't believe she was spending that much time in the restroom and they would probably send someone in to look for her. She only hoped that they wouldn't find the note she had left too quickly or she was sure they'd be able to spot her. Quickly getting out of her disguise, she stuffed the sweatshirt and hat back in her bag just as the elevator door was opening.

Sari left the building and headed for the nearest cash machine. She figured she didn't have much time before they noticed she was gone. There was something about the chief that she didn't trust. Something about how he had dismissed her didn't feel right. Now, all she wanted to do was to put as much space between her and the police.

Spotting a cash machine, she took out as much money as she could from each of her credit cards. She realized how bad it would look; it would look like she was trying to flee the law, but right now she knew she needed money to survive. Once this mess was cleared up the police would surely understand her reasoning.

She stuffed the money in her pocket and headed for the greyhound bus station. She didn't know where she was going, but she had a spooky feeling that they would be after her and she wanted to put as much distance between her and them as she could. They say that lightning doesn't strike twice, but right now, she felt sure that she had managed to get caught up in exactly the same situation that had caused her to miss her planned vacation.

*****

Slamming his door, Jason let out a slew of swear words. Damn it. He should have known that her 'Thank you' really meant 'Goodbye'. He couldn't blame her, what was Chief Harrison thinking? 'Do you have someplace you can stay?' What the hell? Damn it! He had promised her that they would keep her safe and the chief had pretty much given her the brush-off.

Sitting down at his desk, he rubbed his hands over his face. *Where the hell could she have gone?* Looking back up, he saw the note taped to his door.

Lt. Kollar,

I'm sorry. I have borrowed your sweatshirt and cap. I'm sure you won't mind since it appears to be the only protect that the Police can offer me right now. Hopefully, I'll be able to return them to you when all of this is over. I'll be in touch. Sari.

"Damn it, Sari, I would have protected you," he whispered. Opening the door, he headed for the chief's office. At least now, he had something to go on.

****

Two hours later, the greyhound bus made a scheduled stop and she got off. She had turned off her location finder when she had stopped at the bank, so she felt relatively sure she couldn't be traced but she still felt very vulnerable. She didn't think she had been followed, but she couldn't be sure. Glancing at her phone, she saw that it was nearly 10:00 AM, and while she was tempted to call her sister again, to let her know what had happened, she fought the urge to place the call as she felt it would be best not to worry her. Not yet anyway. She had called her sister from the payphone at the greyhound station and had let her know what had happened. They had decided that it would be best to keep their communication at a minimum, both agreeing that it would be safest that way.

Pulling a card out of her pocket, she decided to call the detective. Walking away from the bus, she dialed the number on the detective's business card.

****

Jason looked up from the report he was reading. "Do you have a moment, sir?" Officer Smith was standing at his door.

Motioning him in, Jason sat back in his chair. "What do you have?"

"From what we've been able to gather, CCTV shows Ms. Manning leaving the station and proceeding directly to the ATM cross the street, where she withdrew funds from five different cards. From there, we aren't completely sure where she went, although there is a possibility that she took a greyhound bus. Destination unknown. Surveillance cameras at the depot did see someone matching her description but we aren't sure which bus she might have boarded. Since then, she hasn't used her credit cards or her ATM card so we don't have any new leads there."

"Well, she's playing it smart," Jason said. "She doesn't know who she can trust, so she's not trusting anyone. Damn it. Let's just hope we catch a break before our hitman does. Thanks John," he added as he reached for his ringing phone. "Kollar here."

"Detective Kollar? This is Sari Manning."

Jason stood up. "Sari. Where are you?"

"I can't tell you that right now. I'm sorry. I just wanted to call you and let you know that so far, I'm safe and that I won't be contacting you again. Not until you need my testimony. In the meantime, if you need to get a hold of me, put up a post on Twitter with the tag, 'Finding Sara'; like the movie. I'll watch for it."

"Sari, listen to me. You don't know that kind of people we're dealing with."

"Maybe not," she interrupted him, "but since your chief didn't seem that concerned about my safety, I decided I should take care of myself."

"Sari."

"You know how to reach me, Detective," she interrupted him, and then she hung up the phone and walked toward the bus.

"Damn!" Dialing the operator, he asked if they could find out where the call had originated. Looking back up at the officer, he said, "She's running scared and damn it, we pushed her to it."

Chicago Tribune

The news article was brief. Just a few lines below the photo from a driver's license:

Divers are searching for the body of a woman believed to have been involved in a fatal accident in Milwaukee, WI. In the early hours of Friday morning, the wreckage of a semi-truck was found on the rocks near the shore of Lake Michigan. It is believed that the truck lost control and plummeted over the embankment, landing on the rocks below in Lake Superior before bursting into flames. A backpack containing the driver's license and other forms of ID belonging to Sara Manning were found near the wreckage. The driver, Mr. John Hughes, was found near the top of the cliff. It is believed he must have tried to jump from the truck before it went over the ledge but was fatally wounded in the attempt. Divers are still searching the area for Ms. Manning's remains.

*****

He reread the article and smiled. It was perfect. Now there would never be an investigation into her murder and his secret would remain safe.

When Millstone had refused to play ball, he had known his only chance to get what he wanted was to have him dealt with. Douglas had never been afraid of eliminating the competition, and that was what he had done.

When he had been informed that there was a witness to the senator's murder, he had called Connelly, who had told him that he would take care of the matter.

He had to hand it to Connelly. His men were good at what they did. How they had managed it, he had no way of knowing, but it was perfect—a tragic traffic accident.

He put his game face on and prepared to reply to calls from the press about the senator's demise and urges to step up his bid for the good senator's seat.

*****

Lt. Kollar reread the accident report. "Damn it!"

Shep nodded. "Looks like Connelly's hitman has gotten away with it again."

Kollar nodded. "How the hell he found her before we did, I've no idea, but I don't like it."

Shep nodded his understanding. The MO fit. While they had no concrete proof, they had seen enough to know that if a high-profile hit had taken place, Connelly was undoubtedly connected.

They had heard there was a hit out for their witness, but they hadn't expected him to be so swift. They both suspected that there was a leak in the precinct and this was just another example of it. They had only just identified that the girl had been seen hitching a lift on the interstate highway and that she was seen accepting a lift from a truck driver. The same truck driver that was now dead, and his truck had crashed in Lake Michigan. The girl's bag, along with her wallet, was found hanging on the cliff, telling them that she too had been in the vehicle when it had gone over the ledge. There was no way anyone could have survived the crash, and the divers were still looking for her remains. So far, they had found her coat, but no body, so it didn't look good. The Great Lakes were infamous for burying their dead, sailors of the shipwrecks never to be found again. He suspected the same would be true here.

The lead investigator in Michigan had relayed that due to the condition of the accident, it was doubtful that even if she had managed to escape the crash, Connelly's men would have ensured she wouldn't have walked away. The driver had been found with his throat slit, which gave them little hope. The hitman would have caught up with her as well.

Looking up at his partner, he held his finger to his lips and started to write a note on the notepad in front of him. "Now we've only one more chance left."

Shep nodded and took the note from him and stuffed it in his pocket. He would burn it later. Their one chance was the woman who had disappeared from his watch over a month ago. The woman had approached them with possible evidence that Stephen Douglas was involved in this crime. But the evidence was missing along with the witness.

Duluth

The B&B she had found had a small cabin with a full bathroom. It was cheap and they took cash. It would serve her purposes well.

Opening the door, she stepped into the darkening room and switched on the light. *Small was right*, she thought as she looked around the room. To her right was the small kitchen that had an efficiency size stove and refrigerator, which sat next to a small table with two chairs. The bathroom was next to the kitchen. Taking a quick peek in, she saw that it did indeed have a shower. How they had managed to fit it in there she had no idea, but it seemed to be in working order. The rest of the cabin held a full-size sleeper sofa (that looked like it had seen better days), a coffee table and an old rocking chair that matched the sofa.

Drawing the blinds, she locked the door behind her and put the bags on the table. First things first, she thought as she opened her shopping bag and pulled out the Clairol hair dye and the scissors, she had purchased earlier that day. Walking into the bathroom, she looked at her long blond hair and wanted to cry. She had worked so hard to grow it out, but she knew that she would need some kind of disguise if she were to be safe.

Picking up the scissors, she took a deep breath and began cutting.

*****

Waking early, she headed out. As usual, she didn't want anyone to see her, and she knew she had a long way to travel before she reached her next destination.

She had flushed her hair down the toilet and she would dump the box of dye when she found a large trash dumpster. She didn't want to give anyone any ideas of what she had done to change her appearance. She felt a little silly, but she didn't know what else to do. She had always been good at playing dress-up for Halloween, laughing when her friends or family didn't recognize her. But this time she knew that if she was recognized, it could mean the difference between staying alive or ending up dead.

Her goal was to hike as far as possible, continuing throughout the night if necessary and not stopping until she could find one of the deer stands, she had seen in previous years. She felt that she would be safer if she could hide up in a tree stand than to just pitch her tent on the ground, but she was prepared either way. The bear spray she had purchased could be used on man or beast.

She knew that she had bought enough food and provisions to tide her over until she reached Silver Bay which should take her about five days to get to. She hoped that by then she would have some kind of indication if she was safe to surface. If not, she would be able to pick up more supplies in Silver Bay and head back on to the trail. She really hoped that would not be the case.

She had hiked the Superior Hiking trail a number of times before and she hoped that it would provide her with a good hiding place. The B&B she had stayed at was located just five miles from the trailhead and, with any luck, she wouldn't run into anyone on the way. It was still dark out, but she kept her headlamp turned off until she was out of sight of the B&B.

While people knew that she liked hiking in the SHT, she hoped that no one would guess that she was still running and that this was where she had gone. It was her only option. She couldn't risk putting any of her friends in danger by hiding out at their places, and she couldn't rent a car without proper identification, which she didn't want to risk either. So, she had decided that she would hoof it.

She had managed to catch a ride to Two Harbors the night before and had hiked the two miles to the B&B. Now, leaving before the sun had started to rise, she hoped that no one would know where she had gone.

Two hours later, she was disappointed at how slow it was taking. She had forgotten that hiking in rough terrain took longer than walking around the countryside. She finally reached the trailhead when the sun was starting its slow rise in the east. Grabbing one of the trail maps, she started down the trail.

It had taken her seven days to reach Silver Bay. Much longer than she had anticipated.

She was tired and she needed a shower. She had been on the trail for over a week and she was exhausted. Walking up to the hotel clerk, she smiled at the look she received. She knew that she looked a little rough, but considering everything else, she really didn't care.

"Hi, I'd like to get a room for the night."

"It's $79.00," the clerk said skeptically.

"That's fine." She nodded. But when he seemed to hesitate, she added, "I'll be paying in cash, if that's alright."

"Oh!" He seemed surprised. "Yah, that's alright. I'll just need you to fill out this form," he added as he pushed a registration form toward her, and then he turned back to the show he had been watching when she had walked in.

She picked up the pen and started to complete the form with the false name and information she had decided to use.

Picking it up, the clerk said, "Thank you, Miss," he looked down at the name, "Smyth, if I could just see some identification."

Biting her lip, she started to explain that she had lost her identification while hiking on the trail. She said she hoped that it wouldn't be an issue since she was paying with cash.

The clerk seemed uncertain for a moment, but since it was nearly midnight, he must have decided that he'd let it slide. "I guess it would be alright."

"Oh, thank you!" her face brightened with a smile. "You don't know how much I appreciate it! I really need to dry out the rest of my gear and call my parents. God, you don't know what I've been through. Thank you!"

As the clerk handed her the keycard, she spotted the local newspaper. The headline caught her eye. "Mind if I borrow this?" she asked.

"Take it," he grunted and then went back to watching the late-night show.

Finding her room, she closed and locked the door behind her, then grabbing the chair, she pushed it up against the door, in the hopes that should anyone try to break in, the noise would alert her. Then she collapsed into a nearby chair.

Rereading the headline, she couldn't believe her eyes:

Investigations into the murder of Senator Millstone on going.

A source at the Chicago police department revealed that there are currently no leads to the murder of Senator Millstone. Last Thursday, the Senator was found shot to death on the roof of the US Bank building.

Police are also investigating the murder of Sari Manning, the woman who had witnessed the murder of the senator. Anyone who may have information concerning the murder of Senator Millstone are asked to contact the Chicago Task Force.

Below the article was a small photo that had her swearing. The photo wasn't a good one, but it looked enough like her to have her worried. She hoped her disguise was good enough and that the clerk hadn't seen the resemblance. This was not good, that she knew for sure. She also knew that she had just wasted $79.00 on a room she could not use.

A quick shower and she would have to be on her way. She couldn't risk the clerk IDing her.

She needed to figure out what her next step would be, but first, she needed to get some space between her and Silver Bay, without being seen.

She would have to make do with whatever supplies she could get from the gas station that was across the road and head back onto the trail, and then she would decide where to go after she was sure 'they' were not following her.

Looking into the mirror, she stared at the light brown color she had chosen just over a week ago, and wondered if all this coloring would make her hair fall out, but it couldn't be avoided. On the off-chance that the clerk made the connection later, she knew that she would have to change her appearance once again. The question was, did she make the change now, or wait until she was well away from the hotel? Glancing out the window, she saw that it was pitch black outside. If she left now, she felt confident no one would see her.

Opening her pack, she pulled out her toiletry kit and walked into the bathroom, closing the door before turning on the light. Inside the kit she found the self-tanning lotion and the other Clairol hair dye she had bought.

Grabbing the scissors from her kit, she stared cutting another two inches from her hair.

An hour later, she studied her new appearance and was happy with the results. She just hoped this new transformation would be enough, and hopefully her new skin color and the dark purple mop of hair would fool the best of them.

Gathering all the evidence of her appearance change, she threw them into the plastic bin liner and stuffed it into her backpack. She would throw them away on her way out of town.

Slipping out of her clothes, she quickly took a shower. As she dressed into clean clothing, she contemplated her next move. She hadn't heard any sirens, so she felt fairly safe that the clerk hadn't called the police, but she couldn't risk it. However, she was dead tired; she told herself that she would take a quick 15-minute combat nap. Laying down on the bed, she set the alarm on the clock radio next to the bed, she closed her eyes and was asleep in moments.

*****

She woke with a start. It took her a moment to determine where she was, and then she tried to figure out what had woken her. Sitting up in the bed, she looked toward the door. The chair looked undisturbed. Quietly getting up, she looked at the clock radio and saw that it was 6:30 a.m. Then she realized that the volume was so low that she never heard it go off. Pulling on her hiking clothes, she slipped back into her hiking boots and pulled the toggles tight. Walking over to the door, she hazarded a glance through the peephole. She didn't see anyone, which was reassuring. Walking back toward the bed, she decided to take a glance outside. Slowly lifting the curtains, she looked out onto the parking lot, and found nothing to be alarmed about.

It had been nearly midnight when she had checked in, and it looked like the clerk hadn't recognized her and he hadn't notified the local authorities. Letting the curtain fall back, she sat back down on the bed and tried to decide what she should do next.

Picking up her backpack, she donned her knit hat, stuffing her hair underneath and then she quietly left the room, making her way down the stairs and out into the parking lot. Glancing back toward the hotel, she hoped that no one noticed her departure, as she made her way toward the nearby gas station.

There, she slipped into the store and gathered the supplies she would need before she hit the trail again.

As she was packing her purchases away into her backpack, it began to rain and she wondered if her luck could get any worse.

"Oh dear, you don't have to start walking in this, do you?"

Looking up and saw an elderly woman standing beside her. Smiling back, she nodded. "I'm afraid so."

The older woman studied her a moment and then said, "I don't usually do this, but would you like a lift somewhere? I live near Tettegouche State Park, and they have some nice camper cabins there. You may be able to rent one, or you could at least wait out the shower in the ranger's station."

"I really don't want to be any trouble," she replied.

"Nonsense, I can't have you getting drenched, now, can I? I wouldn't be able to live with myself!" Nodding toward a blue Ford Fiesta, she added, "That's my car, come on." Then she lifted her purse over her head and walked quickly to the car.

She smiled at her luck, picked up her backpack and followed the woman to her car. Throwing her backpack in the back seat, she quickly got in the passenger seat. "This is very kind of you. I really appreciate it."

"I'm Clara." The woman extended her hand.

"Jane," she lied. "It's nice to meet you, and thanks again for the lift. I was planning on hiking to Tettegouche and camping there for the weekend, so this is perfect. I guess I should have checked the weather report before I headed out this morning," she added by way of explanation.

As Clara started her car, she said, "I have a granddaughter about your age. She's a hiker too and I'd feel badly if someone didn't help her out if she needed it. She lives in St. Paul and goes to the university. She's going to be an elementary education teacher. She'll make a good one too. She's very patient."

Smiling back at the elderly lady, she relaxed back into her seat. She knew from previous experience that the ride to Tettegouche would be a short one, but this would give her the head-start she needed and she felt very grateful to the woman next to her.

"How long does your granddaughter have left before she graduates?"

"She's in her second year, but she hopes to get her master's degree so it will be a while yet. She's planning on coming back here to do her student teaching, and will be staying with me in the fall. I'm really looking forward to that. It will be nice to have the company."

"Are you originally from Silver Bay?" she asked, trying to keep the conversation moving. She hoped that Clara wouldn't ask her any questions about herself. She didn't really want to lie to the lady, but she didn't want to make her vulnerable either. While she didn't think anyone would find out that she had gotten a lift, she didn't want to chance it either, and decided that the less Clara knew about her, the better.

"I'm from Iowa originally, but I met my husband up here and we decided to live here."

"Now that sounds like an interesting story."

Clara smiled back. "Well, I suppose it is."

Turning her attention toward the gentle woman, she relaxed as Clara launched into her lovely story.

After Clara had dropped her off at the ranger station, she headed off toward the Superior Hiking trail. The rain had abated a bit and she hoped that she'd be able to make some good time on the trail and reach the second campsite indicated on the map by nightfall.

She knew that she would be well ahead of anyone who may be following her, but she kept looking back to make sure that no one was behind her.

Several hours later, she reached her intended campsite. It was still very light out and a glance at her map showed that another campsite a few miles ahead. Wanting to put as much space between herself and the cities, she picked up her pace.

*****

Sitting sat back against her backpack, she listened to the rain pour down on her tent. She loved that sound. It always relaxed her.

She had found the third campsite just after dark, but had decided to continue up the path until she found an area off the trail that her tent could easily fit in. It was her basic principle to camp only in designated sites, always being conscious of the 'leave no trace' philosophy, but drastic times called for drastic measures and she had taken a deer path several yards off the main path and had found a site well hidden from the trail.

After quickly hanging her food pack, she had put up her tent and she was now sitting in her tent contemplating her next move. As she saw it, she really had only one option. The people who were after her were obviously professionals and she couldn't afford to trust that the police would be able to offer her any kind of protection. After all, how could they have even known she was a witness, if it hadn't been for someone at the police station?

She knew what was at stake; if she was caught then the people who had murdered the senator would kill again. She also knew that there wasn't anywhere that she would be completely safe.

She thought of her family and how much she missed them, but she knew in her heart that for their safety, there was only one thing she could do. She would have to remain on the run, possibly indefinitely. Taking a deep breath, she decided that she would have to take a page out of one of the spy thrillers she liked to read and find a way to reinvent herself.

She had already changed her hair color, now she would have to change her name, her personality…everything. She would have to become a new person. Someone not even her own sister would recognize. She felt her breath hitch and allowed the tears to fall. She missed her sister and the thought of never seeing her again was heartbreaking.

Wiping the tears from her face, she pulled out her trail map. She estimated that it would take her another two weeks of steady hiking to reach Grand Marais, and then another week before she would reach the Canadian border. From there she would decide what to do next. She could stop on the way for more supplies if needed, but she felt that it would be best to keep to the trail as much as possible to avoid running into anyone who may be looking for her.

She would have plenty of time to perfect her new personality. She had watched enough thrillers to know that she would have to make the transformation as complete as possible. She couldn't afford to slip up.

Sitting up, she took out the notepad she had bought at the gas station and started to make a list of her personality traits. Her likes and dislikes and the things that people would associate with her. Then she made a list of characteristics that were the complete opposite, but traits that she felt she could pull off.

First on the list was her name, which she knew would have to be the first item to change. While her own name wasn't exactly a very unusual name, she didn't think it would be a good idea to stick with it. God only knew how long she would have to keep up this charade and she realized that it would have to be a name that she wouldn't easily forget.

Putting a line next to her name, she decided to leave that alone for now, and then she concentrated on the rest of the list.

Going over her list, she realized that some of her habits would be easy to disguise, while others would take considerable practice. Her choice of clothing, as with her hair, could easily be changed, as could her profession. She had already begun to lose some weight from all the hiking and her body was toning up nicely. This, she realized, she could use to her advantage. These were the easy changes. She also knew that some of the changes she would have to make would take some practice, but she felt it would be worth it, especially if she wanted to fully adopt her new persona. Setting her notebook down, she carefully considered who she would become.

Slipping further into her sleeping bag, she decided she would start working on her new personality tomorrow morning. Tomorrow, she would be…Who? She decided she'd think of that tomorrow.

Chicago

It had been nearly 2 months and he still didn't have any more leads on what might have happened to Kiera Davidson. The woman who had claimed to find something that accused District Attorney Stephen Douglas of blackmail. But without her testimony, or the evidence she had brought to their attention, the case was stalled.

Kollar pulled Shep into his office. "We need to talk, and it's a conversation I don't want the chief knowing about. Is that alright with you?"

Shep nodded in agreement. "Does this little conversation have anything to do with our missing witness?"

Nodding, he replied, "She seems to have disappeared, and it's not looking good."

"There's something else. I'm not sure, but I think there may be a leak in the department."

Frowning, Shep asked, "You think it's the chief?"

"I don't know." Kollar shook his head, "I can't put my finger on it, but something just doesn't feel right. First, the woman comes to us with the claim that Douglas was blackmailing the senator, and goes missing while we are taking her statement, and then the chief pretty much dismisses our key witness to the senator's murder."

Shep nodded, "And then there's a hit sent out on the witness. How they found out about her being on the run so quickly, I'll never know. All we know for sure is that her apartment was gone over by a professional. They must have found something that got her killed. Not to mention that the chief is convinced our little informant was also killed, and like Miss Manning, her body just hasn't been found."

Kollar shook his head, "Something in my gut tells me she's still alive. At least for now. It's all very fishy; and then there's the fact that those photographs and the sketch artist's composite disappeared." Kollar added, "I know we didn't imagine the photos with the envelope in them."

Shep paused a moment. "If it's not the chief, then it's someone else in the department who is close to the case."

"I agree," Kollar replied, "I also think that we're going to need some help on this one. This is definitely the big league and personally, I can't help thinking that we should be calling in some back up. The chief wants to keep this in the department. Frankly, I think it's a damn political move, but as you said, I can't be sure there isn't more behind it."

"Listen, I have a couple of connections with the bureau that I could call and ask if they'll do some nosing around."

"That's not a bad idea." Kollar lowered his voice, adding, "Listen, I have an idea that I know where Ms. Davidson could be, but we need to keep this very low key. If the chief or one of his lackeys is working both sides of the fence..." he let the sentence hang.

Shep nodded. "I know. They get wind of this and we could be making our wills out early. Not to worry. The guy I'm thinking of calling knows how to work under the radar."

Standing back up, Shep had his hand on the door when he turned back toward Jason. "Be careful. We won't have anyone watching our back on this one, and I'd hate to lose a good partner."

Kollar nodded.

"Good," Shep said as he left the room.

Kollar knew that something was not right. Too many things had gone wrong with the investigation and he knew that someone in the department was on the take. He had already contacted the DII and they had begun an investigation, but that wasn't going to help him find his witness. He had a hunch and if he was right, then he knew where he could find her.

After speaking with Shep, he met with the chief and told him that he needed some time off. He decided to come clean, at least partially, explaining that he felt that he was frustrated with the case and he felt that he could be losing his edge.

"I should have known she would bolt, and knew… well, you and I both know that that whoever killed the senator probably got to her as well. She died because we didn't do our job. We didn't protect her," he said out of frustration.

Chief Harrison nodded. "I suspect you're right. But damn it, don't take this all on your shoulders. We were all there and none of us copped that she was going to run."

Jason nodded, but looked unconvinced.

"You're a good cop, Jason. Take some time to get focused and then get your butt back here. I need you."

Jason slowly got up from his seat.

"What are you going to do?"

Jason shrugged. "I'm not sure, all I know is I've got to get out of the city."

Scribbling something on the pad of paper in front of him, the chief ripped the sheet from the pad and handed it to Jason. "Here, I've got that cabin up near Duluth, you're welcome to it. You could do some fishing; catch up on your reading…" Then reaching into his desk drawer, he pulled out his keys and took a key off the ring. Throwing it to him, he added, "Take a few weeks to get your head straight and then get back here focused. Hell, you've earned a vacation."

Jason studied the key in his hand and was about to refuse when the chief added, "That's an order."

Nodding, he pocketed the key and said, "Thanks."

As he turned to leave, the chief added, "There's a 10-year-old bottle of scotch in the cabinet. Help yourself, but I'd like it replaced before you leave."

"Will do," Jason promised as he left the office. As he left the office, he saw the chief reach for his phone.

After the door to his office was closed, Chief Harrison waited for the number he had dialed to pick up. "I have another job for you." He nodded into the phone. "I know the terms." He nodded again, and then added one more word, "Kollar."

*****

Jason rubbed the back of his neck as he slowed down to turn into the drive that led to the chief's cabin. It hadn't taken him long to put together a bag of clothing and he had made it to the cabin in just under 4 hours.

After dropping off his bag, he had headed to the nearby Mom & Pop store where he bought two bags of groceries. Bachelor food, as his mom would put it—frozen pizzas, jars of pasta sauce, pasta noodles, boxes of cereal and bags of chips. He also grabbed a 12-pack of beer and a bottle of JD.

Then he asked where he could buy some fishing bait.

"What do you need?" the elderly man behind the counter asked as he led the way to the side of the shop where there was a small refrigerator.

"A couple of containers of night crawlers and some leeches if you have them."

The shop owner nodded. "You'll want some minnows as well," he informed him, and went about fishing out a dozen minnows from a bucket next to the fridge.

As he paid for his purchases, he had casually dropped that he was staying at the chief's hunting cabin, and the shop owner nodded. "The chief usually keeps the cabin well stocked, but if you run out of anything, just let us know."

*****

The cabin was small, but efficient with a small porch off the front.

By the scratch marks on the floor of the porch, he guessed that the porch usually held two Adirondack chairs, which had been brought in the cabin in preparation for the winter.

40

Jason opened the cabin door to see that it opened into the main living area. Looking around, he saw that the cabin itself consisted of three main rooms—the kitchen, the living room and the bedroom—and it had a bachelor feel about it.

It was an open design, with the kitchen and the living room forming one living area with a large fireplace separating the two rooms.

An old worn sofa, a battered reclining chair and a round kitchen table with four wooden chairs made up the bulk of the furniture. The aforementioned Adirondack chairs sat pushed up against one of the walls making the room appear smaller than it actually was.

On the wooden coffee table were outdated hunting and fishing magazines and the old 24" TV had seen better days. Jason even wondered if he could get any of the local TV stations on it.

Next to the reclining chair, in the center of the wall, was a large fireplace with a healthy stack of hand cut logs next to it. On the wall over the television set, was a gun rack with one shotgun and two fishing rods.

The bathroom was basic, with a small shower, toilet and a single sink. The bedroom was small, but the chief had managed to fit in a full-size bed and a dresser.

His assessment of the cabin took only a few minutes. It was a learned habit of his to take in everything about his surroundings. He supposed it was due to his years on the force. Turning from the bedroom, he returned to the kitchen and put his groceries away. Then he grabbed a beer and sat down at the kitchen table. Grabbing his case notebook from his coat pocket, he began to thumb through his notes.

There had to be something that he was missing. It was here, in his notes, he knew it. He had brought a large sketchpad with him and he retrieved it from his bag. Sketching had always been a hobby of his, but now he needed the large sheets to help him draw out the case details.

Jason thought about what he had said to the chief, about Sari probably being found by the hitman. The odds had always been against her, and he doubted the crash had been an accident. But the chief's reply hadn't exactly told him anything either. Something told him that the chief was involved. The photos held the answer. He was sure of it.

He needed to find out who had access to the file and work back from there. Someone knew something, but wasn't talking, and he didn't have time to let the DII use their 'delicate' methods to learn the truth; Kiera Davidson's life depended on it. He knew that she too could have already been found by the hitman, but he had to look for her all the same. His intuition told him that she was still out there, somewhere. The fact that there hadn't been a trace of her, gave him hope that there was still a chance she was alive. He had been looking into a series of murders and he believed they were connected to Connelly, a known crime boss who, it was rumored, had several highly qualified hitmen in his employment, and Jason had reason to believe that Connelly was the man Douglas worked with to fulfill hits on Douglas' bidding.

By the evidence collected from the murdered victims, it appeared that his MO was to always have evidence of the deed. As Kiera's body had not been found, it meant that no evidence had been provided, which gave Kollar the hope that she was still alive.

Looking back over his notes, he confirmed that he had already checked the logs, but as expected, they didn't shed any light onto who has taken the USB stick. He had reviewed the CCTV footage from the evidence room, and it had shown obvious tampering, but there were no unusual finger prints on the tapes. Whoever had grabbed the USB stick had been careful.

Jason made a list of who would have access to the CCTV, and who would have the knowledge of how to alter the tapes. The one name that kept coming up was the chief's. But that was all he had to go on.

Picking up his cell phone, he put a call through to the sergeant in charge of the evidence lock up, and asked who else had requested access to the evidence, on or around the time the photos had gone missing. The man said that the only other name on the docket had been Gene Wilkins, who just happened to be the chief's brother-in-law.

Hanging up the phone, he let out a string of swears words. *Damn it! The chief had to be involved.* There were just too many coincidences. But proving it was another matter.

First things first, he needed to find Kiera—if she was still alive. Now, her testimony would be the only way they would be able to get Douglas. Laying out the map he had bought at the store, he tried to find the name of the lake he had seen in the photos, the photos he had seen at Kiera's apartment.

Something woke him.

Reaching for his weapon, he chided himself. He was in the bleeding woods, there were plenty of sounds that he wasn't used to in the city; any number of wild animals that could break the silence and wake him from his sleep.

Listening carefully, he thought he did hear something in the distance. *Probably just an owl or a wolf,* he surmised.

This damn case really had his nerves on edge. He hadn't gotten any closer to finding the girl, and he certainly hadn't found any proof that the chief had anything to do with the missing photos. He had one more lead to follow up on. Hopefully tomorrow he'd find something that would tell him what had happed to the girl.

Setting his gun back down on the night side table, he rolled onto his back and tried to drift off back to sleep.

Tomorrow I'll know where she is, he thought, as the bullet hit him in the temple.

The man entered the cabin and grabbed the detective's notebook. Thumbing through, he found the information he needed, and then slipped it into his coat pocket. Stepping into the kitchen, he lit the oven and then blew the flame out, leaving the gas running.

The initial blast rocked the house. The second blast leveled the house and sent the place up in flames.

Chicago

He had expected the call.

He had read about the accident and he knew that he would be the one they would call. Johnnie had worked hard to establish his reputation and it was irrefutable.

In history, he would have been known as a tracker, a bounty hunter. He preferred to be known as a finder.

With his new assignment, he began his research. He'd find the girl, whatever it took.

Grand Marais

When Tara Wind first arrived in Grand Marais, she checked into a local B&B and made her introductions. She needed a job and she was counting on the older couple who ran the place to spread the word of her arrival and her desire to settle down in Grand Marais. Tara explained that she was an artist, jewelry being her medium, and that she was interested in getting a job as a bartender or a waitress to pay the bills until her artwork took off.

Within a few days, she was introduced to Billy Johnson, the owner of the local VFW bar, who told her that he was looking for a bartender to help him out a couple of nights a week. He also informed her that he had an apartment for rent above the bar. He promised that the place was clean and the rent was cheap if she would be willing to put up with the late hours. The job paid in cash, which suited her just fine. "I'd rather not have to open a bank account," she explained, "My ex works for the IRS, and well, let's just say that I'd rather him not know where I'm living."

"A real son of a bitch then," Billy grunted. Tara nodded. "No problem. If you aren't worried about benefits, then I can give you a little bump in the wages." Holding out his hand, she shook it as she accepted the position and the accommodations. She started working that evening.

She had bartended during her college years, and enjoyed it. However, creating jewelry had long been an interest for her, and now she had the time to turn her passion into a career. As soon as she got her first pay, she bought the tools she would need. Setting up a work area in her apartment, she spent the first month building up her stock. Then she had some business cards made and posted them wherever she could think in the hopes of attracting some business.

Things were going well too. Within the first month, she had managed to complete a few pieces and she had made arrangements with one of the local merchants to display her work at their shop, giving them a small percentage of the sale. The money wasn't great, but it did allow her to start building up her savings.

By the end of the second month, she had managed to build up a small amount, and after buying herself a few items of clothing and a bicycle to help her get around, she felt that she could start to relax. Everyone in town seemed to accept who she was, and she was beginning to believe that she would be safe again.

*****

Tara was in the local grocery store doing her weekly shopping, when she stopped by the noticeboard to see if any of her flyers had been taken, she saw an ad that caught her attention. Someone was looking for someone to rent one of the cabins just on the outskirts of the Gunflint Trail. Dialing the number listed, she called the number and arranged to meet the owners within the next hour.

Mr. and Mrs. Clyde Smith were an elderly couple who have decided to spend their winters in Florida, and they wanted to make sure that the pipes wouldn't freeze in their absence. They had decided to rent the place, with the provision that if they wanted to use it in the summer, the tenant would have to move out.

The cabin was beautiful and exactly what she was looking for in the way of a retreat. She explained her situation, and she said that she would be happy to watch the house for as long as necessary. "I work at the VFW during the week, but I can definitely stay here on the weekends, and I can stop by a couple of times during the week." Adding that she would keep an eye on the premises and that she would let them know of any problems that arose. Luckily, the Smiths seemed to like her and they rented the place to her. That weekend, she moved some of her things into the cabin.

*****

Sitting back against the soft rustic sofa, Tara took a sip of her coffee and looked out over the small lake that the cabin was situated on. She loved it here. The peace and quiet was a welcome change from the noise of town. Glancing down at the newspaper she had bought earlier on her trip into town for provisions, she thumbed through the paper looking for her horoscope.

It had been over four months since she had rented the cabin, and she had developed a good routine. Sundays were her days to sit back and relax. To read the Sunday paper and to just relax. It had long been a habit of hers to read her horoscope first, before delving into the depressing news of the day. However, today a headline caught her eye and made her break tradition.

Chicago

FBI Field Agent James Hogan's phone rang and he picked it up while still glancing down at the report he had been reading.

"FBI."

"Is this FBI Agent James Hogan?"

"Yes, how can I help you?"

There was a pause at the other end of the phone. James looked up from the report and listened carefully to the silence on the phone. He could hear the woman taking a deep breath.

"Miss?"

"If someone disappeared. Not because they were running from the law or creditors or anything like that… but for their own safety, when would it be safe for them to resurface?"

"That would depend on the situation. Can you be more specific?"

"Not really," was her reply. He could almost hear her biting her lip.

"Ok, can you tell me if the person or reason they were hiding from is still an issue?"

"I don't know. That's the problem. They are still alive, but…" there was a pause, "I believe they are in prison and won't be let out for a very long time."

"Well, then I'd say the person could feel safe enough to surface. That is unless the person in jail has connections on the outside that could pose a threat."

"What do you mean?"

"Well, assuming you are not referring to someone involved with organized crime, I mean, if it was someone just involved with a small gang, or an ex-husband who had sympathetic friends—"

The woman interrupted him again, "And if it was someone involved with organized crime?"

"Well, depending again on the individual and the circumstances surrounding the reason for the disappearance, I suppose the person may need to consider the possibility that a contract could be put out on them."

Again, there was a long pause. "And how would someone know that?"

Now the caller had James' full attention. "Do you have information about one of the individuals we are currently investigating or have recently convicted? If so, we can—"

Again, she interrupted him, "No. This isn't about that, at least not that I know of; this happened about six months ago."

"Where, exactly?"

James could hear her hesitation. "Chicago."

"Douglas," James whispered to himself, but she must have heard him.

"I'm pretty much screwed, aren't I?" he heard her say. He began to reply, meaning to suggest a meeting and protection when he heard the dial tone. She had hung up.

"Damn!" Standing up from his desk, he called out to the man who had transferred the phone call to him. "Any ideas where that call originated?"

The agent shook his head in the negative. "What's up boss?"

"Trouble," James answered. "Get me the Douglas case file."

"You got a new lead?"

"I've got trouble," was James' reply, and then his phone rang again and he glanced at the number, hoping it would be the woman again. It was a number he recognized, and he knew it would be about the Connelly case.

"Sam, what have you got?" he answered abruptly.

"I have a possible lead on one of the victims. It's a long shot, but with your permission, I'd like to run with it," the caller seemed to be whispering.

"What have you got?" James asked.

"It's what I don't have." James could hear the frustration in his voice. "Listen, it's not safe to talk right now. But I need to do a little research under the radar. If you know what I mean."

James nodded. He knew exactly what the man meant. "Just keep in touch." He added, "But if you get anything solid, I want to hear about it. Is that clear?"

"You'll be my first call," the man replied before he hung up the phone.

Whatever the lead was, James knew that there must be trouble attached to it. Otherwise, there wouldn't be any need for the secrecy, and it also meant that there was possibly a leak in the department; otherwise, the agent who had called him wouldn't be going out of the regular chain of command.

Then he picked up his phone and dialed his superior's phone number.

Grand Marais

It was her day off and she decided to stop in at the library to check the internet. Despite the usual quiet, Tara found the staff members huddled in conversation. Tara couldn't help but overhear one of the librarians talking about a tall, dark handsome stranger in town asking questions about a runaway.

Tara was immediately suspicious. She hadn't seen anything in the paper about any runaways in the area, and while she wanted to ask the librarian about the man, she decided that it was best not to draw any attention to herself. Logging off the computer, she decided that perhaps it would be best to take some additional precautions just in case.

Leaving the library, she headed back to the cabin.

When she had first moved into the cabin, she had decided to keep the cabin a secret. She had hoped that it could be a refuge. A place where she could be herself, without worrying about someone snooping into her past. As a precaution, she had also decided to use the cabin as her launch point should anything go wrong in town. From here, she would take daily trips into the Superior Hiking trail, and she had started planning an escape route should the need arise. Stocking up on supplies, she had been placing 'caches' along the trail to aid in her escape, and as the months went by, she had gotten into a nice routine. On her days off work, she would hike further into the trail, setting up a number of 'base camps' that she could hide out in, should the need arise.

She had been careful not to leave any trace of who she was, dealing only in cash, but now she wondered if perhaps her past had finally caught up with her. While she always hoped that she was just being overly cautious, she felt certain that the men who were after her would stop at nothing to find her, and she must be ready for anything. Now it looked like that day might just have arrived.

Glancing at her watch, she noticed that she still had a few hours before she was due at work. There was a few more things she needed to do before work, but as she checked her equipment, she felt sure she would be ready should she need to head out on the trail.

*****

Federal Agent Samuel Johnnie had already spoken with the owner and the other barmaid at the VFW. He had shown them the photo of the woman he was looking for, careful not to mention her name, and neither of them had recognized her but said that maybe Tara Wind, the night girl, might know something. He had confirmed the time she would be on her shift and said he'd be back.

When she got to the bar, her boss Bill Johnson approached her and told her that the FBI were looking for a runaway, and that the man would be back to ask her some questions. Tara shrugged her shoulders and said she would be on the lookout for him. Grand Marais was a small town, and she knew most of the people who frequented the establishment.

She had been on her shift for two hours, when the man walked into the bar. Tara knew at once it was the man everyone had been talking about. He was about 6'4" tall and large. Not fat, but muscular and most definitely handsome. No wonder every woman in town was talking about him. He had introduced himself as FBI, but Tara decided she couldn't count on it. He had a dangerous look about him that made her feel cautious. Besides, the thugs who would be after her could easily fake IDs to get the answers they needed to get her; to kill her. She also knew she had to be 100% sure before she ran again. Pushing aside the urge to seek him out, she stepped behind the bar and got stuck into work.

About an hour later, the FBI agent finally decided to make his move.

Siding up to the bar, he motioned to her and asked her for a beer. After she had poured him a draft and set it down in front of him, he held out a photo and asked, "Have you seen this woman around?" he asked in an obvious Texan drawl.

Tara looked him in the eyes, flirting, before taking the photo between her knuckles. "Who wants to know?" she asked seductively.

"FBI Agent Johnnie," he replied.

Looking down at the old tattered photo, she studied it for a moment before saying, "Pretty girl. What'd she do?" She looked up as seductively as she knew how.

"Just a runaway," he replied.

Shaking her head, she glanced back at the photo. "Sorry, I haven't seen her, but then again, if she's a runaway, I doubt she would be in a bar."

A man down the bar hailed her attention. Handing the photo back to the handsome agent, she added, "Good luck finding her, Tex." Then she went off to help the other customer. Tara tried not to look back at the tall man still standing at the bar. She hoped she had fooled him and that he had not seen though her disguise. When he finished his beer, he threw down a few dollars and headed for the door. Tara was busy with another customer but she knew that before he left, he looked back at her before walking out the door.

Tara gave herself a mental shake. The photo had been an old one, but even she could see the resemblance. She knew what she had to do. He may not have IDed her, but she also knew that she was no longer safe. She had to move on, and that made her angry.

Tara worked until closing and then she walked up to the apartment to settle in for the night. She had done this for the past four months. She knew the routine by heart, but tonight she took extra care in doing it right. She took her time when she got into her apartment, walking around, pretending to prepare for bed. She even went as far as undressing just on the other side of the drawn shade, her silhouette showing her every movement. Then she crawled into bed, turned off the bedside light and laid down on her bed.

She lay there only a minute before carefully slipping out of the bed. She quickly downed the clothing she had dropped next to the bed and snuck out the backdoor that led to the street. However, instead of heading the direction of the street, she headed for the roof and slipped over the edge to the adjacent building, climbing down the fire escape to the alley below. From there, she skirted her way to the back alley and made her way down the street to the post office three blocks away where the 4-wheeler she used to get to the cabin was waiting for her. She took care to ensure that no one had seen her and that no one had followed her. She was sure of that.

She was smart enough to know that despite her precautions, the handsome man who claimed he was FBI would probably be able to find her. But she was prepared for that too. She had had months of worrying, planning, and strategizing. She wouldn't let some Texan ruin everything for her.

She pulled off at the crossing and headed up the long path to the cabin. While the crossing was well hidden, she hoped that the snow that was starting to fall would hide her detour.

*****

It may have been cold outside, but she had started a fire in the pot belly stove that had warmed the enclosed front porch she was sitting in. She was sipping a beer when he arrived. She hadn't heard him. It was more that she 'felt' him. Taking a deep breath, she willed her nerves to calm down. If she had been wrong about him, if he was the assassin hired to kill her, she hoped she would be able to deal with him. If he was the FBI agent, she hoped that she wasn't making a terrible mistake.

"You're trespassing," she said when she saw his tall form in the shadows of the house.

"Mmm," he grunted and stepped out into the porch light. The snow was really coming down now, and she was sure that he had had a hell of time driving in it. "You own the place?" he asked slowly.

She glanced over at him. "A friend of mine does. But you already knew that—and you're still trespassing."

Tara looked back to study the lake and the falling snow. The wind had started to pick up and the cold wind was blowing at a good 20 knots. "I doubt you came all the way out here just for a social call, not to mention that the weather doesn't seem to be travel-friendly. You want a beer before you tell me why you came all the way out here in this godforsaken weather?"

Tara finished the beer that was in her hand. Reaching into the bucket next to her, she took the top off a bottle of beer, quickly added two tablets to it, before pulling it out of the bucket and holding it out in offer as he opened the porch door. Then she grabbed another beer for herself and settled back into the rocking chair. The porch had a wood-burning stove that she had fired up while she was waiting for him. It was good and warm in the porch now, and she hoped that would help set the mood for what she had in mind. She couldn't be sure that he would have found her, but despite the short time she had spoken with him, she had gotten the impression that he was the type of man who wouldn't be fooled too easily.

Agent Johnnie took the beer from her and sat down on the small daybed, the only other seat available in the small porch. The stove felt good, he had to admit that. The temperature had already begun to drop and while he had long grown accustomed to the cold winters and could tolerate it, the warmth felt inviting. He took a long draw off the cold beer before settling his eyes back on her.

She had done well, he thought to himself. He knew she was the woman he sought, but the woman in front of him showed no sign of her true self. Her transformation had been complete.

Almost.

Her looks had changed; the hair color, the make-up. Even her clothing was much different from anything that his target would have chosen.

Shy and demure. That was how everyone he had spoken to described her. Tara Wind was anything but shy. Seductive, that would be how he would describe her now.

Nevertheless, he had noticed some discrepancies. He had watched her earlier as he had sipped his beer at the bar. He had notice, for instance, that she had never really smoked the dozen or so cigarettes she had lit. She had only puffed on them once to get them lit, and then 'played' with them until they had burned out. Most people wouldn't have noticed and would have thought she was a chain smoker.

Or the way she had carefully paused before laughing at a joke or replying to a question when conversing with one of the patrons. She was reminding herself to act as Tara, not as the girl who laughed quickly at jokes and who had had a quick response to everything. She was naive. At least that had been what he had been told, but Tara seemed to know every trick in the book. Just about every characteristic of her former self had been carefully removed. She must have worked hard to become Tara Wind, and he admired her for that. But now the game was up.

Tara felt unnerved by Agent Johnnie's stare but she had continued to look out at the falling snow. She took another sip of her beer, hoping that it would encourage him to do as well. She had guessed at the amount of sleeping pills to add to the liquid when she had prepared it for him. She knew he was a big man, but she didn't want to cause him to overdose. She just needed to knock him out for a few hours while she got away. Reaching over, she put another log in the wood stove and stoked the flames up a bit. Then leaning back in her rocker, she looked over her beer at him and said, "Take off your coat. Stay a while. I really don't think you'll be able to drive back in this blizzard, and as much as I don't usually have house guests, I can't exactly have you driving off in this shit."

Sam continued to stare at her but then shrugged out of his winter coat.

"While you're at it, would you mind taking off your boots? I really don't think the owners would appreciate getting water stains on their new rug."

Glancing out at the storm, he thought, *What the hell. I guess I can't take her out of here tonight in this blizzard. We should be fine here for the night.* Reaching down to unlace his boots, his head spun a little and he sat back up. Tara was still looking out at the snow falling. She was pretty, he decided; despite the ridiculous color of her hair. Leaning back against the back of the daybed, his boots forgotten, he took another draw on his beer. Yes, she was pretty. He had thought so when he first saw her photograph. Pretty but naïve is what he had thought. But now, he saw a different woman. Still pretty, but definitely not as naïve as he had been led to believe.

Tara glanced over and watched the handsome man lean back on the daybed, his beer leaning on his belt, and she waited. He had taken about 3 or 4 long draws off the beer and she felt sure that the drugs were beginning to work their magic. She said a silent prayer that they weren't too potent and that he would simply have a nice long nap, but not a fatal one. When the bottle started to slip from his fingers, she gently pulled it from his hand and set it down on the table between them and then she waited ten minutes more before she began to move.

Studying the man, she wondered briefly if perhaps he was with the FBI, and if so, had she just made a big mistake? But she couldn't shake the feeling that if he was the FBI, wouldn't he have brought the police with him to bring her into custody?

First, she added more wood to the fire and put a warm blanket over him. Then she drew down the bamboo shades that lined the porch. No one walking around the outside would be able to see him. Then she hurried to change into her hiking clothes and left via snowshoe to her hiding place.

She woke with a start.

Listening into the darkness, she tried to determine what had woken her, and for a brief moment, she wondered where the hell she was. As a snowflake settled on her cheek, the events of the last few hours came back to her.

Base camp two.

She had been so exhausted when she had gotten there, she hadn't taken the time to check the tarp above her and now it was evident that one of the tie downs had come loose and she would be soaked if she didn't correct the problem. Reluctant to leave the warmth of her sleeping bag, she began to slowly unzip it when she heard something just below her. Tara held her breath. While she felt sure that her treetop hiding place couldn't be seen from below, she didn't feel as confident now that she had hid her tracks as well as she should have. The sound came again to her left and she breathed a sigh of relief. They were moving off. It was probably just a deer or some other harmless wild animal.

Getting out of her sleeping bag, Tara spared a glance out of the tree fort she had built a few weeks before. The snow was still falling steadily, and she once again felt fairly confident that her tracks would be covered. As she reached up to secure the tarp, she wondered if she shouldn't pack up and head out for camp #3. She had been very meticulous in planning her escape. Creating several campsites to hide out at, but now she was feeling uneasy. Relocating to another state and changing her persona, now seemed to have been the easy part. However, they had found her, and she wondered if this new game plan would be just as easy to follow. She frowned as she looked out into the darkness. She thought about the man she had drugged, lying back at the cabin. She hoped he would be ok, if he was who he claimed to be, the FBI. But she couldn't chance it.

Tying off the rope to secure the tarp, Tara was satisfied that it would stay secure and that it would provide adequate shelter for her. Once again, she toyed with the idea of packing up and going to her next campsite, but she was tired. Bone-tired.

She had left the cabin quickly after she was completely sure that the man who claimed to be FBI was asleep. The snow was falling heavy and she switched on her headlamp and followed the GPS coordinates. Her snowshoes traveling lightly over the new snow and she glanced behind her several times throughout the night and was satisfied to see her tracks disappearing beneath the new falling snow. Her route led her to the lake and to the canoe, she had stowed away a month earlier. She was glad that it was only the early part of November and that the lake wasn't frozen solid. Otherwise, she would have lost valuable time snowshoeing around the lake and her trail may have been picked up more easily. She slid the canoe into the frigid water, breaking the thin layer of ice that had begun to form on the edge of the water, and she started off across the lake. There were two portage sites recorded on the lake, but she knew of a third one. It was an old logging site, and she set her GPS for it, and then paddled off in silence.

After carefully hiding her canoe at the overgrown site, her route had taken her to her first camp, where she had taken only the time needed to verify that her supplies were intact and well hidden, before continuing to Base Camp Two. It had been well after 3 AM when she had finally reached the camp; a tree fort she had built only a few weeks before and after climbing up the spikes she had secured there, she had pulled out her sleeping bag and crawled into it. She was asleep in moments.

Now, standing next to her sleeping bag, she weighed her choices. The snow was still falling steadily, and while she was exhausted, she decided that she should take advantage of the snowstorm and she quickly packed up her sleeping bag.

*****

Sam turned over and felt the rough wool blanket against his face. His eyes popped open. The chair where the girl had been sitting was vacant, and the porch was flooded with light. Sitting up, he glanced at his watch and saw that it was 10:15…in the morning. "Damn!"

He stood up quickly, but had to grab the table next to him as he felt a dizzy spell wash over him. What the hell? And then he spied the bottle of beer on the table.

She had drugged him. "I'll kill her," he muttered under his breath. Right after she testified. Then he would surely kill her.

The snow outside was still falling and he knew that finding her trail would not be easy. He took a quick survey of the cabin. Where had she gone? He didn't have much time. The hearing was in two months and with the price that had been placed on her head, he knew he wouldn't be the only one looking for her. They had collected quite a bit of evidence against Connelly already, but with the witnesses and evidence disappearing, he knew that now time was of the essence. He had to find her and get her before someone else did.

Angry, he turned to head back to his truck when he spotted a magazine, and then he had his answer. Reluctantly, he reached into his pocket and pulled out his cell phone. The man at the other end answered at the first ring.

"She's on the run again. I'm going to need a few things," Sam clipped into the phone. He nodded at the man's reply and ground out, "I know what is at risk!" With that, he clicked the end button on his phone. "I'm going to kill her," he said again as he headed out the door. But he had to hand it to her, she was full of surprises.

Sam locked up the cabin and headed into town. He would need to pick up a few supplies before he set out after her.

*****

Tara stumbled again, and realized that she needed to get some rest. She had managed only a few hours of sleep and she was past exhaustion. If she didn't get some rest, she would start to make mistakes and she couldn't afford to do that.

Glancing down at her GPS she noted that Base Camp Four was about a mile away. Shaking away the fatigue, she picked up her pace, determined to get there as quickly as possible.

*****

Sam's phone rang just as he reached his truck. Looking at the caller ID, he wasn't surprised by the number that came up.

"Hello?"

"Have you found her yet?" the man on the other end of the phone sounded impatient.

"Not yet, but I will," was Sam's response.

"Listen Johnnie, I don't have the time for you to mess up."

"I won't mess up," Sam growled.

"I want her out of the way. Do you hear me? You have one week. If you can't get to her by then, I'll call in someone who can get the job done right. I can afford to get the best, and I'll do it!"

"I am the best!" Sam grounded out, and then hung up the phone. "Asshole!"

Checking his watch, he hit his speed dial. "It's Johnnie," he said to the man who had answered. "He's making threats again." Sam listened to the man on the other end of the phone and then added, "Yeah, I agree. We've got to get to her before they do." Nodding into the phone, he replied, "Don't worry. I'll get the job done." Then he hung up the phone, started up his truck and headed back down the road toward Grand Marais.

*****

Tara rolled over and tried to ignore the pounding in her head.

She had gotten less than six hours of sleep in the last three days and her body was rebelling. Everything hurt—her head, her back, her feet… She didn't think there was one inch of her that didn't hurt.

Looking at her watch, she saw that it was nine o'clock in the morning. She should get moving. If the man who claimed to be FBI Agent Johnnie was on her trail, she couldn't afford to waste valuable time. Especially if he was the hitman sent to kill her. If he was with the FBI, she realized that if he had found her, then anyone who was looking for her would be able to find her, and she couldn't take the chance on getting caught.

Unzipping her sleeping bag, she quickly pulled on her winter gear and packed up her things. Her next camp was eight miles away and it would be well after dark before she reached it. It was taking her longer than she had anticipated in making each of her campsites. She was moving slower because of the snow and fatigue. She just hoped that she was still ahead of the man following her. That is if he had figured out where she had headed.

Thinking back to his handsome face she somehow knew that he was indeed on her trail. He had a look of confident determination etched into his face, and she really didn't relish meeting up with him again. She was sure that drugging him would have put him in a bad mood. Not that she could blame him. It had been her only option; but she doubted he would see it that way.

Picking up her backpack, she shrugged it onto her shoulder and then climbed down from the deer stand where she had spent the night. Then, checking her GPS, she headed off down the path toward her next waypoint.

*****

Sam picked up his pace. He was sure he was on her trail, and now that the snow had stopped falling, he was seeing definite signs of her. He had seen signs that she had stumbled on the trail. She was getting tired; that was obvious. If his calculations were correct, she had been hiking pretty much non-stop since she had drugged him, a fact that still irked him.

He had found evidence of campsites, and he realized that she had been planning this escape for quite some time. *Smart lady.* He had to hand it to her; she had managed to slip past him and had spent the last few days and nights hiking through some pretty rough territory. His research told him that she had hiked the Superior Hiking trail in the past, but he had never taken her to be this hardy. Then again, when someone's life was on the line, one tended to go to some extraordinary lengths trying to stay alive.

Checking his map and the GPS, he verified his location and the tracks he was following verified his suspicions. She was heading toward Ely via the Boundary Water Canoe area. Another smart move, considering it was a protected area and the only way around it was by foot or canoe. He knew that Ely was approximately 114 miles from Grand Marais. That is, if you were driving in a car. But the young lady he was tracking was on foot and traveling the backwoods. At 8 miles a day, it was going to take her roughly 15 days to reach Ely. He estimated that it would take her a bit longer than that. He had half a mind to double back, drive to Ely, and wait for her there. But she had surprised him once, and he wasn't going to count on her sticking to the route he had determined. He would continue to track her, and with any luck, he would catch up with her before she reached Ely. Before she reached civilization.

*****

Checking her GPS again, Tara verified that she was heading toward the Kekekabic trail. When she had begun her journey, she had thought she would stay in the BWCA, using the wilderness as cover. But now she was running low on supplies, and the Kekekabic trail would allow her to travel much faster, and with luck, she'd find some place to stock up.

Her research had shown a few vacation B&Bs near the trail, and she hoped that they would still be open for the season. If not, she might have to break into one of the cabins that were scattered around the area to find some provisions; an option that didn't exactly sit well with her. Her list of offenses was adding up, and she really didn't relish a stint in jail.

Picking up her pace, she wondered again if the FBI agent had figured out where she had gone and if he had followed her. Looking back, she could easily see evidence of her trail, and she realized that if he was on her tail, it wouldn't be hard for him to find her. Her only hope was that she had covered her tracks enough at the start, and that he wouldn't have guessed her plan. One thing she was sure of, he would have had to go around the lake and find her canoe to be on her trail now, and that would have taken him considerable time. If nothing else, she could be sure that he was a few days behind her. Hopefully, that would be enough time for her to get away.

*****

The cabin looked deserted, but she knocked and called out to make sure. "Hello? Is anyone home?" Tara waited and knocked twice more before she decided to break the window. While she hated the thought of breaking in, she realized that she had no other choice. She had walked around the cabin twice and hadn't been able to find any hidden keys, and she needed to get in out of the weather. The storm had picked up and she was sure she was facing blizzard conditions.

Stepping back, she raised her walking stick and punched it through the lower right windowpane. The glass broke instantly. Using the edge of the pole, she knocked the remaining glass away, and then carefully reached in and unlocked the door. Stepping into the porch, she pushed the door closed, and then she looked around for something to shove through the broken window. The snow was already starting to fly in, and she knew that she needed to close up the hole as quickly as possible. Spying a pillow, she stuffed it into the opening and stepped back to see if it would hold. It would, at least for the time being. It would do until she could find something more permanent.

Turning, she surveyed the porch. It was small, but well looked after, containing an iron post daybed, a café table with two chairs and a small bookshelf. Walking up to the cabin door, she crossed her fingers that it wouldn't be locked. She really didn't want to have to break another window. Luck was on her side and the door opened easily. "Hello?" She called out again. She really didn't think anyone would be there, but she didn't want to risk surprising anyone.

Stepping out of her boots, she stepped over the threshold and closed the door behind her.

The room was chilly, but she was relieved to be out of the storm. Taking off her backpack, she tried the light switch and was relieved to see the overhead light come to life. Then she started walking around the room to assess the area. She found a note on the refrigerator that gave instructions on how to bring the cabin to life, and she set about making the necessary adjustments. First, she found the heating control and turned the dial up a few notches to start warming the cabin. Then locating the basement door, she made her way down to the hot water heater and turned the appropriate knobs as the list instructed. Hearing all the faucets come to life told her that she had done everything correctly. She decided that she would let the water run a little while to clear the pipes.

Next to the water heater, she found a washer and a dryer, which she decided she would take advantage of as soon as the place warmed up. Walking in the next room, she found a small sofa, a television and another door that led outside. Next to it, she found a basket with the remains of firewood. She would need to stock up on some firewood, and glancing outside, she was glad to see a large pile of logs not too far from the cabin.

Walking back upstairs, she completed her tour of the cabin, turning off the faucets as she came upon them. In all, she found two bedrooms, one bathroom and a very large living/dining area.

In the porch, she found a pantry stocked full of various canned fruits, vegetables and miscellaneous other food items which would sustain her. In the kitchen, she found more staples, and the freezer even held some edible items. At least she wouldn't starve.

Grabbing her boots, she returned to the basement and ventured back out into the storm to retrieve a healthy supply of firewood.

Closing and locking the door behind her, Tara felt a sense of accomplishment as she surveyed the large stack of firewood that was now lining the basement wall.

Removing her boots, she left them by the door to dry, picked up the firewood basket and carried it up the stairs. After verifying that the flute was open in the fireplace, she started to build a fire and within minutes, she had a warm fire burning. Sitting back, she took off her coat, she was pleased to find that the room was starting to heat up.

After retrieving her boots from the basement, she set them on the rug by the door to finish drying, and hung her coat up on a coat tree that she found next to the door.

Then she went in search of a hammer, nail and something to cover the broken window. She found the supplies she needed in the porch closet and went about repairing the window.

Looking in the pantry, she located the flashlight and spare batteries she had spied earlier and then grabbing the wet pillow that she had used in the window, she verified that the porch door was locked before heading back into the cabin. Placing the wet pillow next to the fireplace to dry, she then began to unpack her backpack. She wanted to get her things washed and dried, and some supplies packed away in case she had to make a run for it again. She felt fairly certain that she wouldn't be found, but then again, her luck in that area hadn't been exactly perfect and she felt it best to be prepared.

Over an hour later, she had her clothes drying in the dryer in the basement, her sleeping bag lay out drying near the fireplace and the rest of her gear was cleaned and packed away. In the morning, she would pack up the food supplies that would be suitable for travel, and then she would be ready.

Feeling a little hungry, she grabbed a few items from the pantry and made herself some spaghetti with red sauce and some mixed vegetables she found in the freezer.

Now, feeling pleasantly warm and full, she slipped into a pair of pajamas she had found in the back bedroom; grabbed a large comforter, and spread it out on the sofa. It felt good laying on something other than the forest floor, and she hoped she would be able to stay there for a while.

Staring into the flames, she felt herself relaxing into slumber. She knew that the fire would burn itself out, so she wasn't worried about it, and she allowed herself to fall asleep, feeling for the first time in weeks that she was safe.

*****

Waking with a start, Tara laid still in the darkness and tried to figure out where she was. The dying embers of the fire reminded her that she was in the cabin she had broken into.

Tara rolled over on her back and tried to fall back to sleep. Hearing a faint sound behind her, she held her breath. Had she locked the doors? Yes, she knew that she had. If someone were trying to break in, they would surely make more noise than that.

Holding her breath, she listened once more to the sounds around her. Hearing the sound again, she realized that it was a faint scratching sound. The storm had picked up a bit, so perhaps it had been something outside hitting against the side of the cabin; a tree branch perhaps. Concentrating on the sound, she was convinced of it. Slipping back under the comforter, she allowed herself to relax.

She was just dozing off when she sensed that she was not alone. Mice. She was sure of it. She had noticed several traps set around the cabin, so it was obvious that they had been seen in the past. The warm cabin had probably attracted them, and brought them out of their hibernation. While she was sure that they would leave her alone, she wasn't so sure that they would leave her sleeping bag and pack alone. She'd have to get up and take care of her belongings. Reluctantly, she stared to untangle herself from the warmth of the comforter.

"I wondered when you'd wake up."

Tara tried to sit up, but found herself pinned down by the handsome FBI agent.

"Oh no, you don't," he said between clenched teeth.

"How did you get in?" Tara whispered, unable to breathe as fear crept into her.

"The basement door," Sam replied. Then as if he anticipated her next question, he said, "Yes, it was locked. But I have some experience picking locks, so it wasn't a problem."

Tara stared back at him and wondered what would happen next. If he really was an FBI agent, wouldn't he release her? However, if he was the man sent to kill her, would he do it quickly and leave or…

"You're here to kill me, aren't you?" She sounded calmer than she felt.

But the answer she sought was not easily gained.

"You drugged me!" He said inches from her face.

The menacing look had her closing her eyes and pushing back into the sofa. She didn't know what to say. "I… I had to," she stammered out.

"Do you know that it is a federal offense to drug an officer of the law?"

Tara opened her eyes and studied the man before her. "You…You're really an FBI agent?" She asked unbelievingly.

Sam leaned back a bit and studied her face. "I said I was." Then he shook his head. Releasing her, he sat back. "I'm here to protect you," he finally answered her question.

*****

Taking her arm gently in his hand, he guided her to sit up. "I think you need to know some things."

Tara allowed herself to be seated, and then she waited. Sam stood up and took off his coat. The cabin had cooled during the night, and she suddenly felt very chilled. Standing again, she walked over to the fireplace and stoked up the fire. Then glancing back, she said, "Would you like some coffee or tea?"

Sam nodded. "Some coffee would be nice, but I'll make it."

She had been on her way to the kitchen, when she understood his reply. Frowning, she stopped and turned back toward him. "I suppose I deserve that." Turning, she walked into the kitchen and started the kettle to boil. "I never really fooled you with my fake name, did I?" she asked quietly from the kitchen.

Sam smiled back at her. "You would have fooled most; but I was determined to find you, and so I was looking for the discrepancies."

Tara thought about that for a moment, but didn't question him further. Turning, she walked into the kitchen and started making the coffee. Glancing back at the handsome agent, she commented, "You may want to take your boots off to dry, and if any of your gear needs drying it might be a good time to take care of it."

Sam was surprised by her suggestion. It was a logical suggestion, but considering the circumstances, her calm behavior surprised him. Accepting the suggestion, he nodded and went about removing his boots, setting them by the door next to her boots and hung his coat on the coat tree.

Then, as she suggested, he unpacked his backpack and laid out his sleeping bag and other items to dry.

66

"There's a clothes washer and dryer in the basement if you need it. My things are probably dry by now."

"I'll do that later," he replied. Glancing down at the steaming mug of coffee she was offering him, he paused. Looking up into her eyes, his question was obvious.

She smiled. "No, it's not drugged. I promise," she added to reassure him. It was then that he noticed that her calm appearance was a ruse. She was trembling.

Sitting in the chair next to the fire, Tara added another log on the fire. Wrapping a throw around herself, she tried to stop her body from shaking. She knew that it wasn't just the chill in the air that was making her shiver.

Sam pulled a stool up next to the fire and studied the woman next to him. While the cabin was a little chilly, he knew that her shivering was not because of the climate. "Are you alright?"

Looking up, she tried to read his eyes. Was he really here to protect her or was that just a line to make her trust him? Taking a deep breath, she took a gamble. "Just be honest with me. Did I make a mistake back there to run?"

Sam put his hand over hers. "I wish you would have trusted me, but your instincts were justified. I really am with the FBI, and I'm here to protect you," he added to calm her.

Tara released the breath she had been holding. Tilting her head, she asked, "Am I still in danger?"

"I need you to trust me," was his answer.

While his reply hadn't directly answered her question, she knew that it was the closest she was going to get. And the answer was yes; she was still in danger.

Looking back into the fire, Tara took a deep breath and decided that she would trust him. She nodded. "How did you know where to look for me?"

Sam put his hand on her arm. "Look at me." Turning her head, he continued, "I found you, because I needed to find you. I studied everything I could about you, and I followed a hunch. The fact that you ran instead of going back to the police told me that me that you were smart enough to know that you wouldn't be safe. It also told me that you wouldn't jeopardize your friends by hiding out at their place. So, I dug a little deeper into your personality and decided that you would probably run someplace you felt safe. I found an old diary of yours, and in it you had mentioned loving the freedom of hiking on the Superior Hiking trail. So, I followed you here."

He paused and took a sip of his coffee. "Then I met a lovely lady named Clara in the Two Harbors post office. She heard my accent and ask why I was in the area. I said that I was looking for a friend who had moved up this way but I had lost her address. Clara asked if my friend liked to camp, and I said yes. She mentioned that she had given a lift to a nice young girl a few months back who was hiking the Superior Hiking trail and that maybe that was the same girl? She added that you had said your name was Jane."

Tara blushed. "I didn't want to put her in any danger," she replied. Frowning, she added, "But there's something I don't understand. I don't have a diary."

Sam frowned back at her. "But…"

"Agent Johnnie, I'm telling you, I've never written a diary in my life." Then it dawned on her. "I'm not who you're looking for," she tried to convince him. "I'm not…" she didn't dare say her name, "the woman who went missing."

Sam studied her a moment. "It's Sam, and I want you to start from the beginning. Tell me exactly who you are and why you are on the run." He was still convinced she was in fact the woman he was looking for, but he needed her to trust him. Getting her to confirm her identity would be the first step.

Tara shook her head. She couldn't risk telling him everything. There was too much at stake. "Please," he added and then he waited for her to begin her story.

Tara looked into his eyes and knew that no matter the consequences that she needed to tell him the truth; at least her part of the story. Taking a deep breath, she began.

"Okay," she agreed. "Where to start? I guess it really began when I was finished giving my statement, and I was asked if there was a place I could stay. I knew instantly that I wasn't going to be offered the kind of protection I had been promised. So, I decided that I had to get out of there. I was a little scared but mostly pisted off that my testimony had been taken so lightly."

"I wasn't sure what to do next, but I remembered that there the greyhound bus station a couple of blocks from the police station, so I went there. I managed to grabbed the next greyhound bus leaving and luckily it was heading north, out of the city. I sat in the back with my head down, nervous that at any moment I'd be caught. I kept waiting for someone to stop the bus, but when no one did, I decided I would just keep on the bus until I had to get off. I didn't know where I was going, but I had a spooky feeling that they would be after me and I wanted to put as much distance between them as I could. I figured, if I was being followed, that they would have jumped on the bus at some point and taken me off. When the bus stopped a couple of hours later, I got off and called the detective to let him know I was still safe. Then I got back on the bus and continued on my journey.

"When I realized the police weren't going to protect me, I knew I had to get out of there, and the first place I thought of was Wisconsin. I used to hike a lot before, well, before my ex decided to ruin it for me." He gave her a questioning look. "That's another story. Suffice to say, he tainted the experience for me. Anyway, I figured it would be a good place to get lost.

"I started to think about all the CCTVs at the bus terminal, and I started to worry that I would be traced to the bus station, so I decided I'd get off the bus and catch another bus or a taxi going in a different direction. I wasn't really thinking straight, because I got out at a deserted stretch of the road. When the bus pulled away, I realized that I was pretty much isolated and alone and then I really felt scared. I started walking, running really and then I spotted a truck and I stuck out my thumb.

"The truck driver stopped and gave me a lift. He was heading up to Superior, and I lied and said it was where I was hoping to get to. We had driven a few hours when we saw a car pulled over up ahead with its hazards on. The driver said that he should stop and see if he could be of any assistance. He was a really nice guy. But as he started to pull over, I got an uneasy feeling. I can't explain it, but I just knew we shouldn't stop, and when I saw the guy who was waving at us, I knew I was right. There was something off about the guy. I told the driver not to stop. I lied and told him that he was my ex-husband and that he wasn't a nice guy; that he was abusive. I pleaded with him, tried to convince him that it would be bad if he stopped. Luckily, he believed me, because as soon as we pulled past, the guy took out a gun and started shooting at us. The driver sped up, but the gunman had a faster car and was behind us in minutes.

"The truck driver said that we couldn't outrun him, but that he had an idea, and then he hit a switch and dumped the trailer behind us. That gave us some time as the trailer now blocked most of the road.

"We drove for another hour and then the driver turned down a dirt road. Pulling over, he said that he had to stop the truck. He thought something was wrong with the tires. He was outside when we saw the other car again, but as he started to get back into the truck, the guy started to shoot again and the driver was forced to run off into the woods.

"I did the only thing I could think of. I got into the driver's seat, backed the truck into the car, hitting it hard, and then I hit the gas and sped off as fast as I could. It was pretty treacherous driving, especially since I really had no idea of how to drive the thing, but I managed to lose him. I was reaching for my bag to call for some help and missed a sharp turn. The next thing I knew, the truck was careening over the side of the cliff, heading for Lake Superior.

"The truck started to tip over the edge of the embankment and I just couldn't correct it. I managed to jump just as it started off the cliff. I lost my backpack and my ID, but luckily, I had stuffed the money I had taken out of the bank in my pocket."

She paused and took another sip of the tea she had made. James studied her for a moment. "You're Sari Manning?" The shock was evident on his face.

"I thought you knew that," she whispered.

"Not until now. Good god," he said as he realized what this meant. But he knew that she wasn't finished with her story. "Go on," he prompted her.

"Well, then I ran. I knew that as soon as it hit the bottom that it would explode. I've seen enough movies to know that, and I wasn't going to be around when the bad guys showed up. I still didn't know how they found me, or why they were after me, but I didn't exactly wait around to ask them. I ran up the hill and managed to hitch a lift to Duluth."

Sari turned and stared into the flames of the fire. "They're still after me, aren't they? And if you could find me—"

"Sari, I wasn't looking for you. By all accounts, you have been listed as deceased. But on the off-chance that someone begins to question that, I'll protect you, and I promise you I won't let anything happen to you. You have my word on that. Besides," he added with a smile, "I wouldn't exactly say you've been the easiest person to track down."

Sari tried to smile back, but found that she couldn't muster it. Looking back into the fire, she tried to push back the fear that was still tightening around her heart. She wondered if she should tell him more. God, she wanted this nightmare to be over.

Sam knew that she needed some time to process everything that they had talked about, so he stood up, saying, "Would you like some more tea?"

"No, thank you," she replied and handed him her empty cup.

Sam wanted to double-check the perimeter and to set up some traps, just in case they did have any unexpected visitors. If he had tracked her down, then there was a possibility that Connelly's men would too, and he would not let that happen.

Not wanting to alarm her, he picked up his dirty clothes bag, mentioned that he would be right back, and then headed downstairs to put his clothes in the wash and to check the doors and windows in the basement. He had managed to sneak in easily, and he wanted to set up a few booby traps just in case. He had learned a lot when he was assigned to Special Forces and so it only took him a few minutes, and when he returned to the main cabin, he found Sari just as he had left her.

Making his way to the back bedrooms, he fastened booby traps to each of the windows he found, and then made his way to the bathroom, where he added yet another booby trap to the window, and used the facilities.

Returning to the main room, he found that Sari had moved to the kitchen, where she was checking the locks on the windows. Turning, she smiled briefly before explaining that she realized that the place probably needed a security upgrade.

Sam nodded.

"I'm assuming that you've been burglar-proofing the backrooms?"

Sam smiled and replied, "I have. Would you like to help with this room?"

She smiled, but shook her head. "I think I'll let the professional do it." Then she walked back to her seat by the fire.

Sam completed his preparations within 10 minutes and felt relatively sure that if anyone tried to break into the cabin, that they would be alerted in plenty of time to act. Glancing at his watch, he noted that it was nearly 3:30 a.m. Turning off the overhead light, he joined Sari by the fire. "It's late, and we both need to get some rest."

She nodded, but didn't move.

"You can take one of the back bedrooms, and I'll sleep here on the sofa," he added by way of direction.

However, she shook her head. "I'd rather sleep in here if that's alright with you."

Crouching next to her, he took her hands into his. "Sari, the cabin is locked up tighter than a drum, and the security devices I've attached would wake the dead."

She gave him a weak smile. "I know. It's just that I'm feeling a bit uneasy right now, and I'm comfortable here."

"I really need to get some sleep, and so do you," he replied honestly.

She held up her hand and stopped him. "I know. The truth is I'd rather have you in the room with me. I know it sounds silly… I'm not asking you to sleep on the floor or anything like that. The sofa is a fold-out, and to be honest, I'd feel safer with you near me." Feeling suddenly very embarrassed, she stammered on, "I'm not trying to be forward or anything…"

It was Sam's turn to raise his hand. "I understand. You don't have to say anymore." Then he stood up and unfolded the mattress hidden in the sofa. It looked clean, and relatively comfortable. "I'll be right back." Then he disappeared into the closest bedroom, emerging with pillows and blankets.

Sari stood up and helped him put one blanket down first as an under sheet, and then they layered several more blankets on top.

As she crawled beneath the blankets, Sam excused himself and headed toward the bathroom to change.

Sam returned wearing a t-shirt and some sweatpants and joined Sari on the fold-out bed. She noticed that he was carrying something in his hand, and when he got beneath the blankets, she realized that it was a gun, and she couldn't take her eyes off it.

Sam reached out and lifted her head to look at him. "This is for our protection." He indicated the gun. "I meant it when I said that I'll protect you. I need you to believe me, and I need you to start trusting me."

Closing her eyes briefly, she nodded. "I'll try."

Putting the gun under his pillow, Sam then lay back and gave her more room on the bed. "Get some sleep, Sari."

Sari studied the man next to her a moment, and then closed her eyes and willed herself back to sleep.

Sam watched her, and didn't allow himself to drift off until he was sure she was fast asleep.

Sari opened her eyes and found herself looking at the face of the sleeping FBI agent. He looked at peace and that felt comforting to her. Slowly moving her legs, she slid out of the bed and made her way to the bathroom.

Being as quiet as she could, as to not disturb the sleeping agent, she brushed her teeth, and washed her face. She would need to take a shower later, but for now, she grabbed a bathrobe she found hanging behind the door and made her way back out into the main room.

It looked like Sam was still sleeping, and so she tiptoed past him into the kitchen to make a fresh pot of coffee and made a box of easy-bake blueberry muffins she had found in the cupboard.

The room was feeling a little chilly, so she made her way to the fireplace and placed a few logs into the fire. Striking a match, she started a few strips of newspaper on fire under the logs. The fire crackled to life and she sat back to warm her hands before the flames.

"Do I smell coffee?"

Sari turned around to find Sam lying on his side, looking down at her. Smiling, she replied, "And blueberry muffins if you are interested."

"You've been busy," he replied.

"Well, you know me; I like to get things done when while you're sleeping." She winked and stood up to get him a mug of coffee.

As she grabbed a couple of mugs from the cupboard, she felt him standing behind her. Sam leaned into her and whispered, "You really shouldn't remind me about that."

She heard the humor in his voice, and relaxed. Glancing back at him, she said sincerely, "I am sorry about drugging you, by the way. I wish now what I had trusted you."

Sam turned her around and looked into her face. "No, it was good that you acted on your gut feeling. Against all odds, you've kept yourself safe and I can't fault you for that."

Sari studied him for a moment. "Thank you for understanding." Then she turned back around and poured them each a full cup of coffee.

Handing him both mugs, she suggested he return to the fire, while she got the muffins out of the oven.

With two plates, a basket of muffins, butter and a knife in hand, Sari made her way back to the fireplace. He had put the sofa back together and had moved the small coffee table back in front of it. Together, they ate the muffins in silence.

Sitting back against the sofa, she asked, "What happens now?"

Sam wiped his mouth and replied, "Well, by the sound of that storm, it looks like we will be held up here for a little while."

"There's a television in the basement. I'm not sure if it works or not, but if it does, it might tell us what the forecast is."

"Good idea. We'll check that a little later."

Sari looked down at her hands before continuing, "And after that? Is it safe for me to go back to the cities yet?"

Sam shook his head. "I wish I could tell you that it was. Douglas and Connelly are determined to keep the evidence at bay, and they have been busy trying to cover up any loose ends. Unfortunately, our sources also tell us that they've made a rather attractive offer to whoever can find both you and another woman named Kiera who is missing, and make sure neither of you testify. The truth is, I wasn't looking for you. I was looking for the other woman, who we believe can provide the evidence we need to prove that Stephen Douglas is involved."

"Kiera?" She asked.

"That's right, Kiera Davidson. She's never been found. Connelly suspects that she's still alive and that's what sent me up this way looking for her. The fact that I mistook you for her tells me that any other hitman they send could make the same mistake."

Sari opened and shut her mouth. She was about to tell Sam the rest of her story, when she realized that he had just said. Sari felt herself grow cold with fear. "What do you mean, Connelly sent you?"

Sam hurried to relieve her fears, "I have been working undercover trying to get to witnesses before one of Connelly's hitmen do. He contacted me because I've built my reputation of finding people."

Sari wanted to believe him. "And as long as no one has found her…" she left the statement incomplete. They both knew the implications.

Standing up, she gathered the dishes they had used, returning them to the kitchen sink. She thought about what he had just told her. "Sam, does anyone know that you've found me?"

Sam had followed her into the kitchen with their coffee mugs. "Not yet. My superiors believe I'm on the trail of Miss Davidson. Why?"

"Why did you start looking up here?"

Sam decided to level with her. "I was initially assigned to investigate both of your disappearances. During my research, I discovered that Miss Davidson was an avid Superior Hiker. After she disappeared, one of the investigating officers in the Millstone murder case, Detective Kollar, was killed in a house explosion. It was thought that he was following up a lead to Kiera's disappearance when it happened."

"Detective Kollar was killed?" She looked ashen. "Did he know where she is?"

"We don't know. All we know for sure is that he took a two-week holiday and was killed shortly after. He told his boss that he was 'going up north for some fishing'. But his partner said that Kollar had an idea as to where Miss Davidson was and was going to follow up his hunch."

"What about his partner? Did he have any more information?" she was worried.

"No. Although he did admit that they both suspected that there was a leak in the department. That is why they used the vacation as an excuse for him to do some undercover work. Miss Davidson had been working with Kollar when she disappeared. The evidence at the crash site was pretty evident that you had died. He took it personally and decided that he wasn't going to use the usual channels to try and find Miss Davidson. It wasn't until he was killed that I was called."

Sari suddenly realized what he had said, and it must have shown on her face. "It's not your fault," Sam whispered to her. He laid his hands on her shoulders in comfort.

"But he was looking for…" she couldn't continue the sentence. Tears were streaming down her face, choking her.

"If you hadn't run, you and he would have both been killed. Kollar was getting too close and Douglas and Connelly would have made sure that anyone getting in his way would have been eliminated."

"Who contacted you?" she asked quietly.

Sam frowned. "Kollar's partner, Detective Shep Wilson."

"Why did Detective Wilson contact you? Why didn't his superior?" She asked suspiciously.

"Shep didn't know if he could trust him," was his answer.

"How do you know that this Shep can be trusted?"

Sam laughed. "I know Shep. He is my brother-in-law. He's married to my oldest sister. Believe me, he's beyond reproach. Besides, he asked me to look into the case and I couldn't say no. That, and I owe him one."

"You owe him one?"

"That's a long story," he replied offhandedly.

But Sari somehow knew that there was more there. "We have all day," she said, waiting for him to answer her question.

Knowing that she wouldn't give it up, he conceded, "Let's just say that he was there when I needed him."

She wanted more of an answer but decided to let it go for now. She didn't know why, but she wanted to know everything she could about this man who was going to protect her.

Pushing away from the counter, she said, "I'm going to jump into the shower, if that's ok with you."

"Of course, I'll take one after you."

Sari nodded and slipped past him. Gathering a change of clothing, she stepped into the bathroom and closed the door behind her.

Sam watched her go. He knew she wanted to know more, but he didn't want her to start doubting him. If he told her that Shep had saved his life when an informant had turned and revealed his location, she would want to know more details, and he wasn't going to chance spooking her. The man he had been guarding had died in the gunfight, but he had survived. Thanks to Shep stepping in front of the bullet that was meant for him. The fact that he had been wearing body armor had been the only reason he was still alive today.

Sari closed the door behind her and leaned against it. Thinking about everything that had been revealed, she realized the implications of it all. She was still safe. At least for the time being, and that was reassuring. Looking around her, she realized that had Sam not been there, she doubted she would have felt safe enough even taken a shower. Pushing away from the door, she opened the drawer under the sink, she pulled out soap, shampoo and conditioner she had discovered on her earlier exploration of the cabin. Setting everything next to the shower, she turned the hot water on, and waited for the water temperature to heat up before turning on the cold water to adjust the heat. Then she shed the pajamas she had been wearing and stepped into the warm water. It felt wonderful, and she was tempted to stand there for the rest of the day. However, she didn't know how long the hot water would hold out, and she didn't want to deprive Sam of a hot shower, so she hurried through her routine.

Turning off the water, she grabbed one towel for her hair, wrapping it around her head in a turban style, and then reached for another towel and started to rub her skin dry.

Fifteen minutes later, she emerged from the bathroom feeling like a woman again. Clean, and ready for just about anything. "It's all yours," she called out to Sam as she slipped into the bedroom to finish dressing.

"Thanks," she heard Sam reply as he passed through the bathroom door.

Picking up the hair dryer she had found in the bathroom, Sari plugged it in and started drying her hair. While her hair was still short, it was fairly thick, and from past experience she knew that if she didn't dry it with the hair dryer, it could take an hour before it was completely dry. Glancing in the mirror, she was struck by the realization that now that she had been found, she would no longer need to dye her hair this ridiculous color. She could go back to her natural blonde locks.

After drying her hair and dressing, Sari opened the door to find Sam just walking by. His hair was still damp from his shower, but he was dressed in fatigues and a 'Go Army' t-shirt. She couldn't help but appreciate the muscular body she saw.

Stopping, he let her exit the room and allowed her to walk back into the main room ahead of him. It was a simple gesture, but it showed that he was a gentleman.

Good-looking and a gentleman. The thought popped into her head before she could check it. *Careful, girl,* she warned herself. She knew that she was vulnerable and realized that she could easily become romantically involved with the handsome agent. But he wasn't there to date her. She reminded herself. He was there to protect her, and she had better keep her mind on track. *Hell, he probably has a wife and five kids, so hands off.*

Walking into the kitchen, she suddenly felt ill at ease and tried to shake the feeling. What was wrong with her? Giving herself a mental scolding, she looked back and saw Sam putting another log on the fire. His back was toward her, so she couldn't tell if he had noticed anything. She hoped that he hadn't. She would be embarrassed if he knew she was attracted to him.

Sam put another log on the fire and grabbed the iron poker to stoke up the flames. Something was bothering him; something didn't feel right. By all accounts, Jason Kollar had been an honest cop. Shep had been his partner for over eight years and he had no doubts about his partner's integrity. In addition, Shep and Kollar believed that there was a leak in the department.

Hell, this entire case smelled of corruption on all levels and he wasn't sure if it would be wise to open things up again.

Stabbing the iron poker into the log that was smoldering in front of him, Sam swore under his breath. If what he suspected were true, then that would also mean that the hitman might have guessed their general location, and that spelled real trouble. He would need to get her some place safe. Some place the hitman wouldn't dream of looking.

Straightening up from the fire, he turned and found Sari staring at him. She blushed and turned to pour some coffee into a mug, but not before he had seen the unmistakable look of… what? Desire?

When Sari had opened the bedroom door, he thought he had seen something in her eyes that looked dangerous. This wasn't good. He hadn't expected her to find him attractive, and given her current situation, any attraction could spell disaster. He needed her to keep focused. Hell, he needed to keep focused, and if this beauty kept sending him those looks, he wasn't sure he would be able to ignore his own feelings. He had found her attractive and yes, desirable from the moment he was handed this case, but he had put his feelings aside and had concentrated on finding her. Correction, he had found both ladies easy on the eyes, but Sari had attracted him physically, which spelled trouble and he needed to concentrate on keeping her safe. He couldn't afford to become involved with her. With the hitman possibly on their trail he would need to keep his wits about him, and getting distracted by an affair was not what he would call a wise move.

Sari was struggling with her own thoughts. *Damn it!* She was sure he had caught her staring at him. She felt like a silly schoolgirl. She was a grown woman, for god's sake. She should be able to keep her hormones in check, and stop fantasizing about that amazing body.

She needed to get some air, but one look at the blizzard outside told her that she would not have to chance to escape just yet. She had spied a bookshelf with several novels in the basement, and decided that they could offer her the excuse she needed to retreat into the other room and the distraction she needed to forget the sexy man in the cabin with her.

Grabbing her fresh cup of coffee, she started for the basement. "I saw some books downstairs I thought I'd like to read. I'll be downstairs," she explained as she started down the stairs.

"Ok," was the only reply she heard, and she was glad when she reached the basement. Switching on the overhead light, she set her coffee down on the small coffee table, and glanced back to verify that he hadn't followed her down.

Breathing a sigh of relief, she frowned at herself. *What the hell was wrong with her?* You would think she hadn't been in a room with a man before. Shaking her head, she walked over to the television set and switched it on. The static that met her told her that the owners had canceled the satellite service while they were gone for the winter. A quick flick through the rest of the channels confirmed her suspicions. Oh well, they would just have to make an educated guess about the storm.

Turning the set off, she turned and started to browse the titles of the books that lined the narrow bookshelf. She finally found an author she was familiar with, and a quick glance of the back cover revealed a story that she thought could hold her interest.

Sitting down on the denim covered sofa, she pulled a wool throw over her feet and started in on the novel.

Upstairs, Sam was still struggling with his own feelings. He would be expected to check in soon, and he wasn't quite sure how to play it. They would expect to hear that he had caught up with Kiera Davidson, and that he had dealt with her. The men who were looking for her were ruthless. They would stop at nothing to make sure that she never testified.

That was why they had called him. He had a reputation for getting things done. But he hadn't counted on this. He needed to think. If he made the wrong move, then everything would be blown out in the open.

*****

Sam picked up his cell phone and dialed the one person he knew he could trust. It rang into voicemail. "It's Sam. I need to talk to you as soon as possible. Call me on my cell." Then he hung up.

Sari watched as he dialed another number. The book she had been trying to read hadn't held her interest as hoped and she had just come up the stairs to see what he was up to.

"I've got her," she heard him saying. "Yes, I know that, god damn it." She could see that he was truly angry. "I said I'd get her, and I did, but there's been a complication. I need another $5,000. Yes, god damn it. I need to rent a car. She obviously had this all planned and now she's driving south." Sam nodded. "I'm on it. No, you don't want to read her obit," he argued. "That would just give the Feds something else to investigate. Fine. I'll bring you a lock of her god damn hair!" He hung up the phone.

Sari had retreated to the cabin door and now she turned and bolted for the outer door.

*****

Sam caught up to her before she had left the porch.

"No, you don't," he said as he grabbed her arm. She tried to pull away, but he flung her onto the small daybed. She tried to kick him, but he straddled her and, grabbing her arms, held them above her head.

"Sari, stop it."

Her fears had abated, and now she felt her anger begin to rise.

"Damn you!" She was tired. She was tired of running, tired of looking over her shoulder, tired of not knowing who she could trust. She had been running on autopilot over the last few days and now that she had stopped, and been caught, she gave into her anger. "You lied to me!" she spat back at him and tried to buck him off her. But he was far too heavy and she found her efforts useless against his strength.

"I said stop it." He leaned into her, putting his full weight on her to ensure compliance.

Finally, she stopped her struggling and with tears in her eyes looked up at him. "Why didn't you just kill me when you first got here? Why the game? Damn you."

"You shouldn't have heard that conversation," he began.

"Why? So, you could just draw me in more? Was that the plan? Get me interested in you? Maybe even fall for you and then kill me?"

"Shut up." He didn't like what he was hearing.

"Maybe get me in the sack first, huh?" She was fuming.

"I said shut up," he roared.

This snapped her out of it and she suddenly felt an overwhelming urge to run. She tried to buck him off her again, but he held fast. Then he realized that she was starting to hyperventilate and she gasped for air.

Pulling her into a sitting position, Sam pushed her head between her knees and told her to breathe. Quietly, he said, "Damn it, Sari, would you just listen to me for a minute?"

He could hear her breathing starting to return to normal and he brought her back into a sitting position.

Wiping a tear from her cheek, he started to explain, "The reason you weren't supposed to hear that conversation is because I knew this would be your reaction." He wiped another tear from her cheek. "Now, are you ready to listen to what I have to say?"

He could read her hesitation as she nodded.

"I'm not here to kill you," he began, and then seeing the doubt in her eyes, he added, "And I'm not here to kill Kiera Davidson either."

"But whoever you were talking to thinks that you are. Or did I misunderstand what you said?"

"No, you got that part right. The man I was talking to definitely wants Kiera dead."

Sari couldn't help the shiver that ran through her. Was this man a murderer?

Her thoughts must have been easy to read. "No, I'm not a murderer. As I told you, I work undercover. The man I was talking to, Joe Connelly, has put a hit out on Kiera, but since she had never been located, I was called in to find her and ensure she was indeed dead. No one knows where she is, not even Connelly, or he would never have hired me to do this hit. I told you the truth when I told you I'm with the FBI. The FBI has already built a fairly strong case against him, and his trial is in two months. Connelly is trying to cover up any lose ends to ensure that he's not convicted.

"About 2 months ago, Shep, my brother-in-law, called me and told me that he and his partner suspected that there was a connection between you and Kiera, how you both went missing directly after making a formal statement at the precinct; and when his partner, Detective Kollar, was killed, he asked for my help. He suspected that someone in the police force was working both sides and he didn't know who he could trust. We've known for a while that Connelly had some people under his thumb on the force, and so I was pulled off another case and told to concentrate on this one.

"I had been working undercover for a while so it was an easy transition. I've been working to gather as much evidence against the man as I could. When we heard Connelly wanted confirmation that Kiera was dead, I knew I needed to get the contract. All I needed to do was to get one of my informants to spread the word that I was available for hire and Connelly took the bait."

He could see that she was hesitating. It was obvious that she wasn't sure if she should believe him. "Sari, if I was here to kill you or even if I had been here to kill Kiera, do you think we'd still be talking?"

She shook her head no. "Sari, I need you to believe me. I made that phone call to make sure that Connelly wouldn't get suspicious and send someone else on the trail. I need to get you some place safe and that is going to take some time. I needed to get Connelly to believe that I was still on the case. Do you understand?"

"I think so," she finally answered. "But who did you call first?"

"A friend of mine in the FBI," he replied.

"And how do you know that he can be trusted?"

Sam smiled. "Believe me. This guy is beyond reproach. If there is anyone we can trust, it's this guy."

Sari considered everything he had told her and she decided that she believed him. What he said had made sense to her. If he had been there to kill Kiera, then he would have already killed her. After all, he had believed that she was Kiera until only a short time ago.

"Ok Agent Johnnie; I'll trust you." *To a point*, she thought. She still wasn't sure if she should tell him everything.

She could see the man visibly relax, and she couldn't help but smile.

"Thank you, Sari, that will make things a lot easier."

She nodded. "Ok, so what's next?"

"Well, first of all, it's Sam, remember?" He smiled at her. "We're going to have to move quickly. I have a couple of phone calls to make first to get some things set up, but then I'm going to get you where you'll be safe. I'm going to need your complete cooperation with everything I set up. And I mean complete. I'm going to need you to do everything exactly as I tell you. Do you think you can do that?"

She took a deep breath. "Yes, I think so. What exactly are you going to need me to do?"

Sam smiled. "Well, first I need to make a few phone calls, and then we need to get moving again."

*****

It has been all arranged. Sam had called in a few favors from a few friends in the FBI and together they had devised a plan that would ensure that Sari would be safe. Sam realized that the only way to make sure that Sari was safe, and by extension, Kiera, if she was still alive, was that she would need to disappear, permanently. The fact that Connolly still questioned if Kiera was still alive made things a bit more complicated, if he wanted to ensure her safety, then he too would need to disappear, which meant he would need to shift Connolly's focus from the ladies, to him. To get Connolly to take the bait, it would mean that he had to put himself in the line of fire.

They had hiked out of the woods and had been met by one of Sam's friends, who had, as requested, delivered a truck for them to use. Then they had driven to Ely, MN, and from there, Sam set his plan in motion.

Calling Connolly, he set the scene. "It's me," he said as Connolly answered the phone.

"Did you get the girl?" Connolly cut to the chase.

"Yeah. I got her. But there's a complication that I hadn't counted on and I want fifty thousand more before I deliver her."

"What complication?"

"She had a friend that had to be taken care of, which was never part of the deal and I want compensation," was his reply.

"You listen to me, you son of a bitch. You aren't going to get another red cent—"

Sam interrupted the man, "Then you won't get the girl," he said simply. "There are other buyers," he added. He knew he had just signed his own death warrant. No one who double-crossed Connolly had lived to talk about it.

"You're a dead man."

"You'll have to catch me first," was Sam's cocky answer, then he hung up.

Sari looked over at him. "Are you sure this is a good idea?"

Sam smiled. "It's perfect. Now, are you ready to go?"

Sari nodded and then stepped into his Chevy Silverado. She was scared, but Sam had explained everything to her and the plan, if it worked, would ensure

83

that she and Kiera would be safe. He had explained that if he could shift the focus off her, and on to him, that Connolly would act quickly. He had a reputation of swift retribution for anyone who double-crossed him. Sam knew that he would now become the target. Now it was all about timing.

He had to get to the rendezvous point before Connolly's men caught up to him. Otherwise, not only would he pay the price, but Sari would as well.

*****

He saw the car coming up behind them. Fast. Looking back in the rear-view mirror, he could now see the man driving the car. He knew him; knew him well. Connelly hadn't wasted time. He had called in one of his top hitmen, and Sam knew that this was it. He just hoped his luck would continue to hold out as he hit the gas.

Duluth Tribune

A Chevy Silverado, traveling at high speeds, crashed into the retaining wall on the North Shore drive, before flipping over the embankment and catching fire.

The bodies of a man and a woman have been found in the burned out car, believed now to have been owned by FBI Agent Samuel Johnnie.

The scene of the accident has been cordoned off by the police, and officials are asking anyone who witnessed the accident to come forward.

Seattle

It had been over a year.

Over a year since Douglas had been sent to prison. He had received two life sentences without the possibility of parole.

Over a year since she had died, and Cheri Wood had started her new life.

Cheri had arrived first in Spokane, Washington, after two weeks of crisscrossing Canada, and then the US by greyhound bus.

When asked, she would explain that it was the cheapest way to see the country, saying that having grown up in Omaha, Nebraska, she had wanted to discover the world, to 'discover herself', but with limited funds, she had settled for a bus trip.

When she hit Spokane, she had taken a long rest, and then she had continued her journey, finally landing in Seattle, Washington. The beauty of the mountains was a welcome sight; a far cry from the flat farmlands she was accustomed to.

She had found a place to rent in one of the older suburbs, a studio apartment situated above a garage that was owned by an elderly couple, Etna and Floyd Jenkins. Cheri had paid two months' rent in advance, plus a $100 security deposit, explaining that she would need to find a job, but wanting to set the couple's mind at ease.

She had found her first job at the local library. It was a part-time job, working a few days a week, but it paid nearly enough to cover her rent of $500 per month. She found another part-time job at the Barnes & Noble bookstore, where she worked afternoons and evenings floating between stocking shelves, tending the cash register and filling in making lattes and cappuccinos in the coffee shop. The money she earned covered her other expenses but still did not give her the extra funds she would need if she wanted to fulfill her dream of traveling the world. So, she had eventually gotten two more part-time jobs. Every other weekend, she worked at the hospital as a housekeeping aide, and then she got a job at a local greenhouse where she worked a few mornings a week. In the spring and summer months, her hours were increased to help with the new growing season.

She enjoyed working with her hands and she toyed with the idea of someday opening her own greenhouse. She had even looked into taking a course at the university and had sent in her application. She hoped to begin classes that fall, but she was still awaiting word.

This was the story she told those who asked. A story she had rehearsed and rehearsed until she nearly believed it herself.

She had made a few friends, acquaintances really, but she didn't open up to people. When asked about her family, she would answer them honestly that she was an orphan. She didn't trust anyone that much. Trust was something that needed to be earned, and she had learned that lesson the hard way.

But, as she reread the newspaper headline, she wondered if now was the time to start trusting someone.

James Hogan Helps Truth Find the Way

Chicago, Illinois Associated Press

FBI Field Agent James Hogan has once again broken into the tightly guarded walls of the Chicago underground and has uncovered links to the Chicago, New York and D.C. crime syndicates, leading to the arrest and conviction of several known crime bosses, several well-known businessmen and a number of members of congress. (The list of convictions is covered in the special edition section.)

Mr. Hogan credited the convictions to the men and women who worked countless hours to see that justice was served.

It is estimated that the conviction has taken a significant chunk out of the drug industry, to the sum of 1.5 million dollars.

But in this reporter's mind, Mr. Hogan is being far too generous, giving credit to everyone involved, but not to the mastermind behind the convictions. Himself.

Mr. Hogan started down the long road of justice over a year ago when he was instrumental in the arrest and conviction of District Attorney Steven Douglas, who was later found guilty of four counts of murder, and seven counts of extortion. It was also discovered that Douglas had embezzled over

Cheri looked up from the article and out at the gathering storm clouds. "The truth always finds a way," she whispered the words to herself. She couldn't tell if the statement gave her comfort or cause for worry.

She had believed that the truth would always save her, and look where that got her. Truth and trust seemed to go hand in hand, and Cheri wondered if now was the time to start believing again.

"Only one way to find out," she said aloud, and then she opened her laptop and started her internet connection.

*****

"Hey Cheri, any chance that you can work late tonight?"

It was Thursday, technically Cheri's day off at the bookstore, but her boss, John Edwards, had asked her to come in to help set up for a guest speaker and book signing. The author, George Bateman, had written the bestseller, "Undercurrent", a literary account of the fall of crime boss, Marco Sylvie.

John had been running around like a chicken with its head cut off for the last two weeks, ever since he had gotten confirmation that Mr. Bateman would be coming to the store for a signing. He had even arranged a high-profile cocktail party for after the signing to be held at the Gallery, an art gallery located next door to the bookstore. The cocktail party was being billed as a charity event for the Seattle Crime Prevention Association.

Cheri knew that the book signing was scheduled for seven p.m., and it was expected that the man would sign books until nine p.m. when the store usually closed. The cocktail party was scheduled to start at eight-thirty p.m., allowing people to arrive early, and thus assuring a packed room when Mr. Bateman arrived at nine-thirty, escorted by John of course.

John had hired one of Seattle's premier catering companies to host the event, and Cheri had helped compile and send out over two hundred invites. Over a hundred people had already replied and John suspected that more would show up due to the recent advertising push.

Cheri figured that John wanted her to work late to clean up after the signing; something she would have preferred not to do, but she could use the extra cash and so she found herself saying that she would work late.

"Ok boss. You want me to close up or something?"

"Actually, I need you at the party. It seems that Mr. Bateman has invited some guests of his own, and I need someone to make sure they are taken care of."

"What? Like do the meet and greet thing, and check their name off the list?"

John cleared his throat, and Cheri knew there was more. "Actually, I kind of need you to do a little more than that."

"Spill it." Cheri laughed at his hesitation.

"I'd like you to get their drinks, make sure they get a fresh drink when they need one, and act as a …" John paused, looking for the right word. "A buffer."

"A buffer?" she repeated.

"Well, only if it's necessary. I'm not really sure it will be necessary, but just in case some of the guests try to get too friendly. I don't want this event to turn into another book signing. I'm going to have my hands full managing Mr. Bateman," John added in explanation.

"Well, Cheri? Will you do it? I'll even give you the afternoon off, with pay, to get ready; and I'll throw in an early bonus so you can get a new cocktail dress."

Cheri laughed. "It seems you've thought of everything."

"Please?" he pleaded with her, and from his expression, she could tell that he already knew she was going to accept. Glancing at her wristwatch, she saw that it was already two-thirty p.m. "Ok, but you better let me sneak out of here now, or I won't have enough time to find something suitable and get back here on time."

"You're a peach." Reaching into his desk drawer, he pulled out an envelope that had her name printed on it. "Here is the bonus, and—"

"You knew all along that I'd agree, didn't you?"

"Well, let's just say that I had high hopes and decided to be prepared," he replied with a smile. "There's also a ticket for the party tonight in the envelope.

You'll need that to get in the door." Cheri took the envelope and waved goodbye as she headed for the door.

*****

It took her over an hour and a half to find a suitable dress, and another hour to find shoes, a wrap and jewelry to match, leaving her barely an hour to get herself showered and be back at the store by 6:30 p.m.

It was 6:15 p.m. when she walked out her door and she jumped on her Vespa and sped to the bookstore. She walked in at 6:35 p.m., and she could see the relief on John's face, until she saw that look slip when she pulled her rain poncho over her head. She had worn her regular work clothing, and not her cocktail dress. "Don't worry, boss, the dress is here." She held up the shopping bag as proof. Heading toward the back room, she added, "I'll have plenty of time to get dressed before we head over to the party."

Mr. Bateman was 'fashionably' late, having discovered Seattle's rush hour traffic, and he strolled in at 7:15 p.m. To his credit, he had called John at 6:45 p.m. to say that he was running late, and John had pacified the growing crowd by offering free coffee. Cheri estimated that there were nearly 100 people there already.

When Mr. Bateman arrived, John made a brief introduction and then handed the microphone to the author.

"Thank you, John. I'm happy to be here, and I appreciate the opportunity to meeting with you all. As you all know, "Undercurrent" was written primarily to expose the different layers that the crime world operates on, and how, with the help, or perhaps I should say, because of the dedication of many to break through those layers, that a good number of the key players have been arrested and are now safely behind bars."

He paused a moment until the applause died down. "My next book, which is due to be published at Christmas, goes deeper into the law enforcements involvement and success in getting these criminals." With a smile, he added, "And yes, FBI Agent Hogan plays a key role in that story as well." He paused, as there were some shows of appreciation from the crowd. "I can see that there are quite a few people here, so I won't delay any longer so that you all have time to stop by before the store closes at…" Looking over toward John for confirmation and receiving a nod, he continued, "9:00 p.m. Thank you and I hope you all enjoyed the book and are intrigued enough to buy the next one."

Handing the microphone back to John, Mr. Bateman stepped back and was awarded with another round of applause. Once the applause died down, John spoke again, "As Mr. Bateman mentioned, the store will be open only until 9:00 p.m., so we would appreciate you keeping that in mind when you meet with Mr. Bateman. Also, as most of you are aware, we are hosting a charity cocktail party directly following the signing at "The Gallery". The doors open at 8:30 p.m. and the party will continue until 2:00 a.m. This is a black-tie event, with proceeds going to the Seattle Crime Prevention Association. Tickets are $150 per person and can still be purchased at the front of the store. Thank you for attending and now, without further ado, I'll let Mr. Bateman get started."

Cheri took the microphone from John and was briefly introduced to the author. "If there's anything you need, just give me a nod," she said as she shook his hand.

"Thank you," he replied. "Maybe you could keep an eye out for my guests to arrive?"

"Certainly," Cheri replied.

"Don't worry, you'll probably recognize them, but I did tell them to stop by the information desk and ask for John just in case."

"And their names are?"

"My fiancée, Linda Nelson," Cheri smiled in reply, "and James Hogan."

Cheri nodded. "I'll keep an eye out for them." Then she stepped back to allow the first customer to meet the author.

The next hour and a half were busy as Cheri tried to keep an eye on Mr. Bateman, to refill his water jug and get him new pens when he needed them. She also helped to funnel customers into an orderly waiting line, all the while trying to keep an eye on the front door, hoping to catch sight of Mr. Bateman's guests as soon as they arrived.

She had just given Mr. Bateman a new pen when she saw Ms. Nelson walk in the door. Leaning near him, she whispered, "I believe your fiancée has just arrived."

Mr. Bateman looked up and smiled in her direction, nodding hello when he caught her eye.

Cheri excused herself and went to meet the beautiful blonde. "Hello, Ms. Nelson? I'm Cheri, Mr. Bateman asked me to keep an eye out for your arrival."

Linda Nelson smiled back at her and seemed a little relieved. "Hi. That was very nice of you. George knows how uncomfortable I am with these public appearances."

"Not a problem. Would you like some coffee or some water? You could wait in my manager's office if you'd like a quiet retreat."

"I don't want to be any trouble," she began, but Cheri could tell that a retreat was exactly what she wanted.

Glancing up at the clock, she saw that it was 8:45 p.m. "Mr. Bateman will be wrapping everything up shortly anyway. There's a private bathroom attached to the manager's office; you can take the time to freshen up before the party."

Cheri guided the lady toward the back of the store and up the stairs to John's office. John kept a supply of bottled water in his small fridge and Cheri retrieved a cold bottle and a clean glass for Ms. Nelson. "Make yourself comfortable, and I'll just let Mr. Bateman know that you are up here. In the meantime," she pointed to a semi-closed door, "that's the restroom. I'll knock before I come back in."

"Thank you again. I really appreciate this."

"Not at all." Cheri waved as she left the room.

Reaching the main store, she caught sight of John and hurried to his side. "Ms. Nelson is up in your office freshening up. Would you mind telling Mr. Bateman?"

"Good, I was just going to wrap this up anyway," he replied and walked up to the desk where Mr. Bateman was signing a book.

Looking up from the book he was signing, Cheri saw him smile and nod at someone toward the front of the store. Turning, Cheri saw whom he had greeted.

James Hogan was as handsome in person as his photos indicated. Swallowing back her nervousness, Cheri went to greet the man.

"Mr. Hogan? I'm Cheri. Mr. Bateman asked me to greet you. Ms. Nelson has also just arrived. She is upstairs in the manager's office waiting. If you'd like to follow me, I can take you to her."

The tall man smiled down at the young clerk. Her nervousness was obvious and he wanted to set her mind at ease, so he nodded his compliance.

Cheri led him through the crowd as John was making his closing remarks, adding that Mr. Bateman had agreed to return tomorrow afternoon, and that anyone wishing to be added to an advanced waiting list, should stay in line and sign the form he was leaving on the desk. Then he too led Mr. Bateman toward the office.

Cheri met the two men at the bottom of the stairs. "John, this is Mr. Hogan." She introduced the man who had graciously followed her. As the two men shook hands, Cheri took the opportunity to excuse herself. "If you gentlemen will excuse me, I need to get ready."

John patted Cheri on the shoulder. "Cheri will be joining us at the party. I've asked her to help play hostess. So, if there's anything you need, just ask her."

Cheri smiled. "But since I don't want to look like one of the wait staff, I'd better get working on my transformation."

Cheri waved goodbye and headed for the storeroom where she had hung her dress. Cheri knew that she didn't have much time, so she grabbed her things and slipped into the employee's restroom, locking the door behind her. Stripping out of her work clothes, she applied fresh perfume and then stepped into her new undergarments. Nearly naked, she studied her face and hair. She didn't usually wear much make-up, not wanting to stand out, but she knew that tonight would have to be an exception. Reaching into her make-up bag, she pulled out some blush, eye make-up and the new mascara she had purchased earlier, and started to put on her face.

That done, she tackled her hair; the angular bob cut didn't seem to offer too many options, but she remembered seeing a hairstyle in a magazine recently that may work. Starting at the longer side, she began to roll her hair along the back of her head, forming a kind of French roll along the base of her head, adding hairpins along the way to secure her hair in place. At the other side, she pulled her hair into a small rubber hairband and then twirled the ponytail into a small bun, securing it with pins. Then she gave her hair a good dose of hairspray, parting the hair on her forehead to soften the look. She was pleased with the results.

Stepping into the black cocktail dress and her shoes, she glanced at the clock and saw that she was running out of time. Opening her evening bag, she pulled out the jewelry she had bought. Ruby-colored earrings and a matching bracelet completed the look.

Stashing her work clothing back in the gym bag, she stepped out of the bathroom and put her things in a corner out of the way.

She took one last glance at the mirror and was happy with what she saw. The dress wasn't flashy, but in the back of the dress there was a single strand of ruby stones that fell down the open back and gave the dress an elegance that she liked.

Stepping out of the storeroom, the whistles and catcalls had her smiling. "Down boys," she laughed at her co-workers.

"Cheri, you look beautiful!"

Cheri turned to thank John's wife, Sandy, for the compliment, but the words were lost in her throat when she saw Agent Hogan staring at her with a look that did not look like disgust.

Finding her voice, Cheri smiled at Sandy. "Thank you, Sandy, you look marvelous yourself." Then mentally taking a deep breath, she asked, "Have you been introduced to Mr. Hogan?"

"Yes, John just made the introductions."

John took his cue and spoke up, "Well, if we are all ready, I suggest we head on over."

As the group began to leave, Cheri realized that everyone was coupled off—leaving her as Agent Hogan's date. Grabbing John's arm, she held him back while the others left the building. "Hey, John, so when exactly did you learn who Mr. Bateman had invited as his guests?" The blush that tainted his cheeks was her answer. "Darn it, John! What did you do, tell the man I'd be his date?"

"No! I swear it was nothing like that. It's just that… Sandy thought it would be a good idea."

Cheri laughed. "Oh, so now you're going to pin the blame on your wife." Linking arms, she steered him out the door. "Don't worry, I'm not going to back out on you, but I am going to make it perfectly clear to the man that no one was trying to set us up on a blind date."

Joining the others, Cheri quickly established herself as the group's waitress and left to retrieve everyone's drink of choice.

She had stopped by the Gallery earlier in the day and had introduced herself to the head bartender, explaining her role and she had been assured that once the initial order had been placed, that she would have no trouble getting prompt service. Her plan worked too, for when she stepped up to the bar, the bartender greeted her and promptly took her order, even supplying her with a tray to carry everything.

Glancing over her shoulder, she caught sight of the group just as the mayor and the chief of police were greeting them. Her order having arrived, Cheri carefully made her way through the crowd and caught Sandy's eye as she approached the group. John had just finished introducing the guests of honor and turned to take his drink from the tray. "A toast; to our guests and to a successful evening."

Cheri rose her glass and took a sip of the sparking water. "To an interesting evening." She heard Agent Hogan's deep voice next to her. Looking up, she saw his glass raised in her direction. Touching their glasses together, she smiled back at him. "Cheers," she said in reply.

The group started to move further into the room and Cheri took the opportunity to slip away to return the tray to the bar.

Downing her glass of water, she asked for another. The bartender once again filled her champagne glass with sparkling water. Thanking him, she turned to find Agent Hogan standing close by. "Agent Hogan, I'm sorry, was there something you wanted? Is your drink alright?"

"Yes, it's fine. Although I don't recall ordering Glenlivet's."

"Oh, sorry about that. I shouldn't have assumed… would you prefer a different brand?"

James Hogan laughed. "No, not at all. I happen to be a fan of Glenlivet's."

Cheri's throat was beginning to feel dry from nervousness and she took another large gulp of her drink.

"Hey, go easy there. The night's just begun."

This time it was Cheri's turn to smile. "Thank you for your concern, but I'll be fine."

Hogan tried to reason with her, "That stuff tends to sneak up on people."

"Agent Hogan," she began to explain.

"It's James; after all, if we are going to spend the rest of the evening in each other's company, we should be on a first-name basis. Don't you think?"

Cheri smiled and nodded in agreement. "James, I think I can safely say that I could drink these," she lifted her glass before continuing, "all evening and I wouldn't feel any effects."

James decided to take another approach. "Care to place a wager on that?"

Cheri laughed. "Oh, you have no idea how tempting that is, but I feel it's only fair to warn you that I have you at a serious disadvantage."

"Oh, and why would that be?" he countered.

"Well, since I have no intention of taking advantage of this situation, I'll tell. This, my dear sir, is not champagne. It's sparkling water."

James laughed. "Thank god you're an honest woman."

Cheri nodded in agreement.

"I take it you don't drink."

"On the contrary," Cheri replied, "how do you think I knew to order the Glenlivet's? No, I just decided that since John asked me to do a job, I would keep a clear head. Speaking of which, I better make the rounds and check to see if everyone is OK in the drinks area."

James took her elbow and guided her through the crowd to join the others. Luckily, the others had been busy meeting people, so their glasses were still full. John caught James' attention and introduced him to one of Seattle's leading businesswomen, Mrs. Shirlene Wousley. Cheri knew from reading the society pages that Mrs. Wousley was a divorcee, but liked to keep the Mrs. title for business purposes. By the way she was oozing out of her dress, Cheri was sure she had come to the event with more than business on her mind. "Mr. Hogan, or may I call you James, it is such a pleasure to meet you." Seeing Cheri standing near his side, she added, "I'll have a dry martini."

The drink order was meant to get rid of her; Cheri knew it, and she wasn't happy about it, she glanced at John for backup, but he just raised his eyes in submission.

"Of course, Mrs. Wousley," she replied, then turned and hurried off. "The nerve of the woman…" She muttered under her breath.

"I couldn't agree more." Cheri heard behind her. Turning, she found James walking up behind her.

Looking over his shoulder, she saw the woman in question in hot pursuit. "Your friend followed you," Cheri said in warning.

But James seemed to smile. Taking her hand, he brought it to his lips, and just as Mrs. Wousley arrived, he said, "Darling, you are my gem. Thank you for taking care of things, but you aren't here to fetch drinks for people."

Cheri pushed the laughter from her voice and took up her part. "James honey, I know that, but I did want to help John out of an uncomfortable situation."

Pulling her toward him, he whispered in her ear, "Is she buying it?"

Cheri gave a throaty laugh. "Honey, behave yourself."

That seemed to do the trick.

"Miss, I'm very sorry. I hadn't meant for you to get the drink; I was just making a statement," Mrs. Wousley lamely explained. Then trying to cover herself, she added, "James, I hadn't realized that you were seeing someone."

"Mrs. Wousley," James emphasized her name, "I'm not in the habit of discussing my personal life with anyone outside my immediate circle. Now, if you will excuse us."

Turning back to Cheri, he slid his hand to the small of her back and guided her through the crowd to where the chief of police was standing.

"Hello James," Chief Koltes greeted them. "I see you got away from Wousley."

Cheri looked up at James for an explanation. "Bill and I go way back," he explained. "We went to college together at Boulder."

"And the stories I could tell," was the chief's reply.

"Not if you care about the stories I could tell," was the quick reply.

The chief laughed, "OK, let's call it a stalemate. So, are you going to introduce me?" he added, looking down at Cheri.

James started to make the introductions, "Bill Koltes, Cheri—"

"Wood," she replied shaking the chief's hand. "It's a pleasure to meet you, sir."

"Sir? Hey, any date of James' can call me Bill."

"Well, then I better call you—"

"Bill," James interrupted her.

"Bill," she agreed with a puzzled look.

Two other men joined them, and as Bill began to make the introductions, she quickly excused herself and made her way back to check on the others. A quick glance told her that she was on drink detail and she made her way to the bar. Getting refills, she made her way back to the group and handed out their new drinks. Snagging a passing waitress, she handed off the tray, first grabbing James's drink and her sparkling water.

She found James still in conversation with the other two gentlemen that the chief had introduced him to. Handing him a fresh drink, she took his empty glass from him and placed it on a nearby table. "Gentlemen, allow me to introduce you to my girl Friday, Ms. Cheri Wood."

"Don't let him fool you, gentlemen. I'm just here to keep him out of trouble," she said with a wink.

"That's a tall order," was the chief's reply and they all laughed.

James saw George heading their way and said, "If you'll excuse us." And then once again, he put his hand around Cheri's waist and guided her away from the group toward George Bateman.

"Hey James, Linda's about ready to bolt. Any chance you can come work your charm? I really shouldn't leave just yet."

"No problem," James replied with a mischievous grin on his face.

George led the way and as they walked up to their group, Cheri stepped up to meet Linda. "Hi! Are you enjoying yourself? I love this gallery; it has a lot of beautiful artwork. In fact, have you had a chance to see the Monet collection yet?"

Linda Nelson seemed to brighten up. "No, I hadn't realized they had pieces from that period."

"Oh, yeah." Cheri tried to sound casual. "If your fiancé doesn't mind, I could show you the collection."

"Go ahead, honey. I know you love that stuff."

As Linda gave her fiancé a kiss on the cheek, George winked his thanks to Cheri.

Turning back to Cheri, Linda also winked at her saying, "You are my savior."

Cheri laughed and linked arms with her. "Let's blow this popsicle stand. Sandy, care to join us?"

"Of course," was her answer.

James watched as the ladies wandered away toward the gallery hall.

George was the first to speak, "That's some assistant you have there, John."

"Yes." John nodded in agreement. "She's full of surprises."

Taking a drink of his scotch, James casually asked, "Has she worked for you very long?"

"About a year; unfortunately, she's only part-time, otherwise I'd have made her my assistant manager by now."

Puzzled, James asked, "Have you offered her fulltime?"

"On a number of occasions, but she's made it clear that she has other commitments. Getting her to come in on one of her off days is nearly impossible."

The conversation turned to other topics, but James could not stop thinking about the young assistant. There was something about her that seemed familiar, but he couldn't put his finger on it.

*****

Half an hour later, the ladies made their way back and Linda grabbed George's hand and insisted that he too go see the beautiful artwork.

Cheri once again seemed to disappear, returning with fresh drinks for the gentlemen.

James snagged a passing waiter and whispered something. A few minutes later, the waiter was back with a fresh glass of scotch.

Taking the glass from the waiter, he handed it to Cheri and took her glass of sparkling water from her. "John, I think Cheri is off duty for the night, wouldn't you agree?"

John nodded in agreement. "Of course. You did a great job, Cheri. Thank you."

Cheri studied the man in front of her. Was he flirting with her, or did he just not want to be the only one drinking? "Thank you," she whispered, raised her glass in salute, and adding, "To an interesting evening." Then she took a sip of the scotch.

It had been a while since she had enjoyed a glass of Livet and she savored the sip. It warmed her instantly and she smiled at the glow of warmth.

Sandy motioned toward the front door. "Oh, oh. It looks like Mrs. Wousley hasn't quite given up."

Cheri forced herself not to look in the direction Sandy had indicated but asked, "What do you mean?"

"She's making a beeline this way," John answered her question.

James put his hand on the small of her back, leaning into her and whispered, "Ready to play your part?"

Cheri looked up into his eyes as seductively as she knew, answering, "Honey, I was born ready."

Reaching up, she toyed with his tie as he looked over to Sandy and John, winking to ensure they played their part as well.

James could sense that Mrs. Wousley was nearby so he knocked the act up a notch. Intimately sliding his hand up her back, he gently caressed the nape of her neck. "Having a good time, honey?" He asked in a husky voice.

Cheri smiled up at him. "I am. You?"

"I couldn't think of anyone I'd rather be with," was his romantic answer. And by the look on her face, it was one which Mrs. Wousley obviously had also heard.

"Mr. Hogan, tell me. Are you in the habit of lying to the public?"

"Excuse me?" James frowned at the woman.

"You lied to me!" She replied bluntly.

"When was that, Mrs. Wousley?"

"You and this tramp are not dating," she spat out in anger.

"First of all, to call this young lady a tramp is defamation of character, and you of all people should be careful about making statements like that. Second, whether or not Ms. Wood and I are dating is none of your business. If it were, I'd tell you truthfully that Ms. Wood is my date this evening."

"Your friend George Bateman claims otherwise."

"My friend, Mr. Bateman, knows that I don't flaunt my personal relationships and would have told you that Ms. Wood was asked to lend assistance as requested by her boss, also true. Now, if you will excuse us, you have insulted and interrupted us long enough." James turned and led Cheri away from the obnoxious woman.

John and Sandy also followed, but not before John gave her a piece of his mind. "Mrs. Wousley, I believe you have overstayed your welcome. I suggest you leave."

"I paid for my right to be here."

Nodding to the approaching security guards, John added, "Your check will be returned to you, on your way out. This is a charity event for violence prevention, your personal attack on one of my employees and a friend of the guest of honor does not fit with the theme of this event. Now, please leave."

The mayor and Chief Koltes had also joined the group. "Chief Koltes, Bill," Mrs. Wousley tried to get the chief's sympathy.

"You are out of line, Mrs. Wousley," the chief replied. "I think it would be best if you were to leave."

Her back was really up now. "What? Are you afraid I'm going to cause a scene?"

"You'd only be embarrassing yourself," was his reply.

This stopped her. She had a reputation to protect, and she realized that her jealous anger had probably already cost her. She'd have to do some damage control later. But for now, she would leave quietly and gracefully.

*****

John and Sandy left to meet up with James and Cheri—who had worked their way to the bar nearest the band. The music was louder, preventing conversation, which was just fine, as far as Cheri was concerned. She was fuming and at the moment, she didn't trust her voice. Taking a long drink of her scotch, she concentrated on the music and tried to calm down.

James could tell that she was fighting for control. He was having trouble controlling his anger as well. Not since his high school days had he experienced blatant jealously like that. It had surprised and then angered him. Her verbal attack on Cheri had been totally uncalled for.

James hadn't said anything to Cheri, allowing her the time to gain control of her emotions. From the look on her face, he couldn't tell if she would scream or cry. Then, to his surprise, he saw a smile begin to form on her lips and then she busted out laughing.

Her laugh was contagious and he found himself smiling.

Cheri turned to him then. "Sorry, but can you believe her? I mean, what a bitch; pardon my French—but could she have been more childish?"

"I was thinking the exact same thing." He laughed. "I don't think anything like that has happened to me since high school, or even junior high."

John and Sandy had heard their exchange and despite their anger, found themselves laughing at the situation as well.

The music slowed and Cheri found James taking her drink from her and leading her to the dance floor.

George and Linda were also dancing and they made their way next to them. "Sorry man. I had no idea she was fishing for information. I must be rusty."

"It's not your fault," Cheri assured him. "Mrs. Wousley was just looking for trouble."

"Yes, I know, but I'm sorry you got the brunt of it."

George and Linda danced off then, leaving them to dance on their own.

"Are you ok?" James whispered into her ear.

Cheri looked up with a smile. "Yes, I'm alright. I can't say that's ever happened to me before, and I hope it doesn't ever happen again, but what is it they say about learning from tough experiences?"

"What doesn't kill you makes you stronger," he answered for her.

"Exactly, and look at me, I'm tough as nails."

James studied her a moment; he still had a feeling he knew her or had met her before. "Who are you? I have a feeling that we've met before."

"Is that your chat-up line?" she teased him. "It's that déjà vu thing," she explained. "I get that sometimes. Someone will come into the store and ask me if I went to their high school or something. I've even been told that I look like some movie star. I think it's the hair," she added with a smile.

"Maybe," he replied, but he wasn't convinced.

Cheri laughed. "Don't stress out about it. I can guarantee that you and I have never met before tonight. Believe me, if we had met before, I would definitely remember," she added with a wink.

The song ended and they left the dance floor to join the others.

George glanced at his watch and then whispered something to Linda. She nodded yes, and then he addressed the group. "I hate to say this, but I think we are going to call it a night."

John looked at his watch as well. "Jesus, it's already 1:30 a.m. I think we had better call it a night as well. Let me get the ladies' wraps," he added, and then left in search of the cloakroom.

"You're staying at the Hilton, aren't you, George?" Sandy asked.

"Yes, we are."

"We can offer you a lift if you'd like. It's on our way home," she offered.

"That would be great, if it's really not an inconvenience."

"Not at all." Then turning toward James, Sandy asked, "James, are you staying at the Hilton as well?"

"No, I got a room at the Marriott. But don't worry about me; I can catch a taxi or something."

John arrived with the wraps and they all walked out of the Gallery together.

"It was a pleasure to meet you both," Cheri said, shaking George and Linda's hands.

"It was nice to meet you as well," they replied, and then they headed to the parking lot with John and Sandy.

Turning toward James, she asked if he would like her to order a taxi.

"How are you getting home?" he asked.

"I'm driving," was her reply.

"Any chance of a lift?"

Cheri smiled. "Only if you don't mind riding piggyback on the back of my Vespa."

"Do you have a spare helmet?"

"Of course."

"Then I'd love a lift."

Cheri smiled and tilted her head toward the back of the museum. "This way then."

Unlocking the seat of her scooter, Cheri pulled out her spare helmet and handed it to James. Pulling on her own helmet, she got on the Vespa and started it up. Then she pulled on her jacket and invited the man to join her on the back of her Vespa. "You're staying at Marriott on the waterfront?"

"That's right."

"Ok, hang on," she said over her shoulder and then pulled the Vespa out of the parking lot.

The hotel was about twenty minutes from the store, but Cheri was able to get there in about fifteen minutes. Turning off her scooter, she slipped her helmet off and hung it on her handlebar. Taking the other helmet from James, she returned it to the storage area under her seat, and then she turned toward James and extended her hand. "It's been a pleasure meeting you." She smiled up at him.

Taking her hand, he held it for a moment. "Care to come in for a nightcap?"

Cheri smiled. "Very tempting; but I had better get going before I turn into a pumpkin."

James smiled back, squeezing her hand. "We wouldn't want that. It was a pleasure meeting you as well."

Cheri gently pulled her hand from his, placed her helmet and got back on her Vespa as James stepped back from the scooter.

Cheri thought for a moment and then turned toward him. "I think I would have enjoyed that nightcap," then she smiled, "but somehow I don't think it would have ended there."

James looked slightly puzzled. "It wasn't all an act tonight," she added before pulling away from the curb and driving down the street.

James stared after her. "Damn," he muttered to himself. What was it about this girl that had his interest sparked?

Walking into the hotel, he stopped by the front desk and requested an 8 a.m. wake-up call and then he took the elevator to his room.

Cheri was busy separating a large Hosta in the back potting area, when from behind her she heard, "So this is where you are."

Cheri looked up in surprise, turned and smiled at the handsome agent. "Hello! What are you doing here?"

"Well, I stopped by the store with George; he had that second signing this morning, and they told me you worked here on Fridays. I wanted to thank you again for playing the perfect hostess."

Cheri looked inquiringly at him. "You're welcome, although you really didn't have to come all the way over here to do that." Tilting her head, she studied him before asking, "Or was there something else on your mind?"

James smiled; the woman was direct. "As a matter of fact, I was hoping that I could take you to lunch or something. I still feel badly about how things developed last night, and since I'm going to be in town for a couple of days, I thought I'd see if you had some time free."

"That's really not necessary. You aren't to be blamed for Mrs. Wousley's behavior."

"I know, but I still would like to show my appreciation."

Cheri studied him a moment and then nodded in agreement. "Ok, that would be nice. Thank you. But I don't get out of here until 2:00 p.m. I could meet you back at the Marriott at 2:30 if that's ok."

"Sounds perfect;" He replied. "Well, I better let you get back to work. See you at 2:30."

Cheri waved a gloved hand and then watched him leave the shop. Something told her that there was more to this lunch then Mr. Hogan let on; but since she'd have to wait to find out, she turned back to the Hosta and concentrated on her work.

*****

At 1:30 disaster struck. The bottom of the bag of fertilizer Cheri had been carrying suddenly split open, covering her instantly. She spent the next fifteen minutes cleaning up the mess and by the end of it she was covered head to toe in mud and dirt. *So much for going directly from work*, she thought and then picked up the store phone and dialed directory assistance.

*****

The phone was answered on the second ring.

"Hello?"

"Hello, is this Mr. Hogan?"

"Yes?"

"Hi, it's Cheri Wood, I'm really sorry to do this to you, but I'm going to have to delay our lunch."

"Is everything ok?"

"Oh yah, I just had a slight accident at work. Nothing serious, a bag of fertilizer and I had a difference of opinion."

James laughed. "Who won?"

"I think I did. But by the state of me, it's hard to tell," she answered with a smile. There was a brief pause and then she continued, "Anyway, it means that I have to run home and clean up first and I won't be able to meet you until 3:30 at the earliest."

"Ok," he answered.

"If you're hungry and don't want to wait, I completely understand."

"What about you? You still have to have some lunch, don't you? Or are you trying to get out of our date?"

Cheri smiled, thinking, *Date huh.* "I could swing by and show you the carnage if you'd like."

He laughed, "No that's alright, I believe you."

"How's this," she spoke again, "you haven't been to Seattle before, have you?"

"Well, I have, but only on business," he answered hesitantly.

"Well, if you allow me an hour to get cleaned up, I'll show you a part of the city you may not have even heard of before. In fact, if you don't mind having a late lunch or early dinner, I know an excellent seafood restaurant that hasn't been overrun by the tourists."

James smiled. "Sounds tempting. You've got a deal."

"Great! I'll pick you up between 4:00 and 4:30 p.m."

Then, just as she was about to hang up, a thought occurred to her. "James?"

Thankfully, he was still on the line. "Yes?"

"Two questions…"

"Go on."

"One, I'm not messing up any of your other plans, am I?"

"Not at all." He smiled, making a mental note to call George and cancel their dinner plans.

"Good," she replied.

"And the second question?" he prompted.

"I'll be picking you up on the scooter. Is that ok?"

His smile deepened. "It's perfect."

"Thank you. I'll see you in a little over an hour. Ciao!" She hung up and hurried to collect her things.

When she got home, she took a quick shower and blow-dried her hair and then she studied the contents of her closet, before finally deciding to wear her green crocheted dress with her brown cowboy boots. After applying some mascara and lipstick, she grabbed a pair of earrings and some silver bangles, and headed for the door. Picking up her jean jacket and her shoulder bag on her way out the door.

Pulling up to the hotel, she found James sitting at one of the café tables situated outside the hotel bar.

Standing, he grabbed his jacket and strolled over to meet her. "You look nice," he said when he reached her.

"Thank you." She smiled at his compliment. "Are you ready to go?"

"Yep, you got a place I can store this?" he added, raising his jacket in explanation.

Once again, Cheri removed the spare helmet and handed it to James. His jacket, she folded neatly into the storage space, then she handed him a small disposable camera. "Just in case you want some snaps."

"Thanks," he replied and then climbed onto the back of her Vespa. After a moment, she pulled away from the curb and headed south, away from the city.

Along the way, Cheri pointed out items of interest, offering suggestions for other sightseeing opportunities.

45 minutes later, she pulled off the main thoroughfare and headed east, toward the coast. Pulling down a small paved road, James suddenly found himself surrounded by dense forest, and then, just as suddenly, the ocean was before them, stretching as far as the eye could see.

Cheri stopped the Vespa and cut the engine. Taking off her helmet, she shook her head to puff up her hair and then she stood and walked toward the side of the cliff.

James joined her. "It's beautiful," he remarked. "How did you find this place?"

Cheri laughed. "A wrong turn. When I first moved out here, I had a job interview to be a caregiver to an elderly woman. I got the directions completely mixed up and ended up here. When I called to explain that I had gotten lost, she wasn't very impressed. Needless to say, I didn't get the job, but I did find a beautiful hideaway," she concluded with a smile.

They stood there staring out at the beauty.

They say that silence is golden, and Cheri didn't want to spoil the moment with casual chit-chat. The roar of the ocean below seemed to be enough.

When James finally looked away from the ocean, Cheri asked if he would like to take a walk.

Cheri locked her Vespa, and then led the way down a path that followed the cliff. As they walked along, James asked her, "How long have you been working at the greenhouse?"

Thinking a moment, Cheri said, "A little less than a year, I think."

"Is that the reason you haven't gone fulltime at the bookstore?"

"One of the reasons," she replied. "I like working there. There's a great sense of accomplishment when you work with your hands. It feels honest."

"And the bookstore doesn't?"

Cheri smiled. "Not in the same way. The bookstore gives me the opportunity to interact with people. The greenhouse takes me back to the basics. It keeps me grounded."

"What did you do before?" he asked.

The question didn't seem as innocent as it appeared, and it teetered on topics that Cheri would prefer not to discuss, so she gave a vague answer. "Nothing really, you know, just odd jobs through school." Then she turned the question to him. "And you? Did you join the FBI right out of college?"

"Pretty much; I was one of the lucky ones, I guess. I put my application in early and got accepted."

"You mentioned last night that you and Chief Koltes went to college together."

"Yes, we both went to the University of Colorado in Boulder."

"Is that where you are from?"

"No, I grew up in Chicago. But I like to ski, so Boulder seemed like a good choice."

"Do you still ski?" She asked.

"Not as much as I'd like, but I manage to get back to Boulder every couple of years."

Cheri ducked under a tree branch and then stopped, waiting for James to maneuver his tall frame under the branch.

Pointing down the path, Cheri said, "See how the path runs down the side of the cliff?"

James followed where her finger was pointing. "Yes."

"See that little shack?" James nodded yes. "That's lunch." She smiled at him. "Come on, it'll take only a few more minutes."

True to her word, they were down the side of the cliff in no time and James soon found himself seated on a wooden chair, at a small wooden table that was facing the pounding waves.

"Do you trust me?" Cheri asked, and James replied, "Well, you haven't disappointed me yet."

Cheri took that as a yes and ordered two house specials and a pitcher of beer.

"What's the house special?" James asked after the waiter had left.

"A slice of heaven," she said mysteriously.

He laughed. "Ok, I'll be patient."

When the pitcher of beer arrived, James poured two glasses full and handed her one of the glasses. "To an excellent tour guide." He raised his glass toward hers.

"And a charming companion," she replied in turn, clinking her glass against his in salute.

Taking a sip of the beer, he sat back in his seat and enjoyed the scenery. "How did you find this place?"

"My landlords recommended it. After I struck out on the caretaker job, I decided to find an apartment and then concentrate on finding a job. I saw an ad in the paper and met my landlords. One night they invited me to dinner and I told them about getting lost and finding the cliff. Turns out they knew exactly where I was talking about, and they recommended this place. I guess it belongs to a friend of a friend or something like that. Anyway, one afternoon I decided to try it out. I've been coming here ever since."

Their meals soon arrived and James was treated to a large seafood platter which had everything from crab legs to oysters Rockefeller.

"Bon Appétit," Cheri said as she picked up a grilled shrimp and took a bite.

The food was excellent, and they spent the next hour enjoying their meal and sharing favorite restaurant experiences.

When the waiter cleared their plates, he asked if they would like another pitcher of beer. Cheri turned to James and said, "I have to drive, but go ahead if you'd like some more."

James shook his head, "No, we're fine," he said to the waiter, who nodded and left to collect the bill. "That was excellent, Cheri. Thank you."

"You're welcome. But do me a favor? If word gets out about this place, I will never get a table. So maybe keep this little gem between the two of us?"

James laughed. "No problem. So," he sat back in his seat, "where to next?"

Cheri smiled. "That's a good question. I guess I assumed you'd have some plans for the evening."

"Nope, I'm all yours for the night."

"Ok…" Cheri sat back and considered their options. "Do you like music?"

"Yes," he said hesitantly, "but I'm not really into that garage grunge band stuff," he answered honestly.

Cheri laughed. "It's not all that bad, but I was actually thinking of the blues. I know a great place that's not too far from your hotel that should be fun tonight."

"Sounds great, I like the blues." Glancing at his wristwatch, he added, "But it might be a little early for a club."

Cheri reached over and turned his wrist toward her to look at his watch, and saw that it was just after six o'clock. "True," she replied, "but not to worry; I have a couple of other ideas up my sleeve. That is if you're willing to put yourself into my hands for a couple of hours," she added with a wink.

James leaned forward. "I said I was all yours for the night." His voice was husky.

Cheri realized the sexual connotation in what she had said and shaking her head, she decided to ignore his reply and laughed. "You may regret saying that, but you've asked for it."

The waiter arrived with the bill and Cheri took the opportunity to excuse herself from the table. On her way back from the ladies' room, she stopped by the hostess desk and bought a bottle of her favorite wine. The maître d put it in a bag from her.

Back at the table, James was just finishing the last of his beer. "Are you ready to go?" she asked.

"Yes. If you'll just excuse me for a moment," he replied and then headed toward the men's room.

When he returned, he found her standing at the water's edge looking out over the sea.

Turning, she smiled and handed him the bag. "A souvenir," she replied. "I just hope you like it as much as I do." Then she added, "It's a tradition of mine. They own a small vineyard and make a great wine, so I usually treat myself to a bottle when I visit. But today, this is for you."

"Thank you, Cheri, you didn't have to do that."

Cheri waved him off. "What kind of tour guide would I be if I didn't provide some souvenirs? And speaking of tours, are you ready to continue on your adventure?"

James laughed. "Adventure, huh? Ok, I'm game, lead on."

Cheri pointed up the hill. "Now for the hard part," she said as they headed back up the hill to her Vespa.

Once back at the Vespa, they took another moment to take in the beautiful scenery, and then they headed back toward the city. This time however, Cheri took a different route, showing James some more points of interest along the way.

Pulling under a bridge, she stopped the Vespa and they got off. Pointing under the bridge, she added, "Our goblin."

Carved into the sand was a sculpture of a large monster, seeming to devour a VW Bug. "Now that's cool," was his reply.

"Here, give me the camera. I'll take your photo."

James handed her the camera and went to stand next to the sculpture.

Cheri advanced the film and noticed that it was already on 20, which meant that he had been busy taking photos after all. She had taken a photo of him near the cliff, and again at the restaurant, but she hadn't been aware that he had been taking any other photos.

Taking the photo, she started to hand the camera back to him when a woman asked, "Would you like me to take a photo with both of you in it?"

Cheri was about to say that it wouldn't be necessary, when James said, "Thank you; that would be nice."

Cheri advanced the film and then handed the camera to the woman.

Standing next to James, she felt his arm go over her shoulder in a casual embrace and she looked up at him. Receiving a wink, she turned and smiled at the lady taking the photo. "Say cheese," she said, and then she took the photo. "That was nice," she said as she handed the camera back to Cheri.

They thanked the lady and then walked back to the Vespa.

Cheri handed him the camera, adding, "I noticed you've been taking some photos. Let me know if you want me to stop the Vespa so you can get a better picture."

"It's fine. You're a very smooth driver, so there really hasn't been the need."

"Thank you, but do let me know if you want me to stop."

"I will," he promised. "Where to next?"

Cheri glanced at his watch again. "Well, I was thinking we could swing by the Space Needle and then head to the bar, if that's ok with you."

"Yah, that sounds good, but I was thinking. I really don't want you to have to drive all night, so why don't we drop your Vespa off at your place and get a taxi? That way you can have some cocktails as well."

Cheri considered his suggestion. "OK, but my place is kind of out of the way. I can leave my Vespa at the Marriott and pick it up in the morning."

"Are you sure?" he asked.

"Oh yeah, no problem. It will actually suit me. I need to come into town tomorrow anyway, and this way I will have my Vespa for later."

"OK, but only if you let me get you a free parking pass, and pay for your taxi ride home."

"You really don't have to do that, but OK, it's a deal."

Parking the Vespa in the hotel parking lot, she retrieved his bottle of wine and their jackets. Then they stopped by the front desk to register her license plate number with the attendant on duty. Handing the bottle to the attendant, James asked that he have it delivered to his room. Then they hailed a taxi and went to the Space Needle.

She had taken the camera off him and taken a photo of the Space Needle as they drove toward it.

At the top of the Needle, they found a small table next to the window and James asked her what she would like. Again, she smiled with a wink, adding, "Trust me?"

James smiled, "Go on then." Turning to the waiter, she ordered two glasses of prosecco.

When their drinks arrived, they touched their glasses together and each took a sip of the sparkling champagne.

Taking the camera out of her bag, she pointed it at James and said, "Smile". Good-naturedly, James raised his glass and smiled back at her. She snapped the photo and then slid the camera back in her bag.

"It's a beautiful view, isn't it?" She remarked as she looked out the window.

"Yes, it is," he agreed.

A vale of darkness was beginning to fall over the city and the view started to fade from sight as the windows began to reveal their reflections instead.

Looking at her reflection, James said, "You really love it here, don't you?"

Cheri turned to him. "Yes, I do," she answered honestly.

"I understand that you aren't originally from Washington."

He saw the subtle change in her face. Her smile remained, but now there was a guarded look in her eyes. "That's right. But I consider this my home now," she replied.

He had the distinct impression that she wanted to change the subject, and her next comment confirmed it.

"I like the peace and tranquility. It's the kind of place that lets you forget the past and concentrate on the future."

But James wasn't quite ready to let it go. "Was there something about your past that you want to forget?"

Cheri smiled and thought, *That's what you get for trying to get one past the FBI.* Then she laughed. "Doesn't everyone? But hey, you're on vacation. Take off that detective hat and let yourself get back into adventure mode."

James conceded, "Sorry, force of habit."

"That's alright," she replied and then steered the conversation into a different direction. "Speaking of adventures, when you said I had you for the night, how late does that mean?"

Again, James winked. "What did you have in mind?"

Shaking her head, she made a mental note to watch how she worded things and added, "No questions. Remember, you are being adventurous. Just answer the question."

Smiling, he replied, "I'm yours until you go home."

"You're sure? You don't have to get up early or anything?"

James laughed. "Definitely not."

"Good. Then finish your drink, we have some blues to listen to."

*****

After the blues bar closed at midnight, Cheri took James to an underground nightclub that was open until 3 a.m.

They talked and danced and to Cheri's relief, he never asked her about her past again.

At 2:30 a.m., they made their way back to the hotel. Stopping outside, she turned to him. "I hope you had a good time. I know that I did."

"I did, thank you. I take it today's tour is over?"

Cheri laughed. "Yes, I'm afraid so. This is Julie, your cruise director, saying goodnight."

James looked down and saw that she had extended her hand. Taking it in his hand, he looked into her eyes. "I'd like to see you again, if that's alright with you."

Cheri nodded yes. "I'd like that."

"Would later today be too soon?"

Cheri smiled. "I don't think so."

"Good. Can I call you a little later to make plans?"

"That would be nice," she replied and then slid her hand from his and reached in her bag for her notepad and a pen. Writing her cell phone number on the slip of paper, she tore it from the pad and handed it to him.

He slid the note into his pocket and then leaned down and gave her a gentle kiss goodbye. "I'll see you in a few hours then."

Cheri looked up into his eyes. "I look forward to it." Then she stepped back and he hailed a taxi for her.

Handing the taxi driver a twenty, he gave her another kiss goodbye and then closed the car door for her.

Waving goodbye, he waited until he saw the taxi turn the corner and then he went into the hotel and up to his room.

*****

Cheri thanked the taxi driver and got out of the car at the end of the driveway. She hadn't had him pull up to the house, because she didn't want to wake her landlords.

Quietly sliding her key in the door, she was just about to reach in to turn on the light when she felt someone grab her from behind and place a hand over her mouth.

"Don't make a sound. You wouldn't want to wake the neighbors, or someone else might get hurt."

Cheri nodded her compliance, as she was pushed into her kitchen. "We want you to give a message to your boyfriend."

Cheri frowned and shook her head. "I don't have a boyfriend," she tried to say against the hand held over her mouth.

Her reward was a slap against the side of her head. "Shut up. We know all about you and Hogan. Now, you're going to tell him to back off the Connelly investigation or more's going to get busted than a few heads. Got that?"

Cheri nodded yes. She wondered whose heads had 'been busted' when she was suddenly struck from behind and knocked unconscious.

*****

Cheri slowly opened her eyes. The blinding headache was her first reminder of what had happened. The second reminder was the fact that she was lying on her kitchen floor.

She waited a moment before she moved, listening to see if the guy who had jumped her was still in the apartment. Satisfied that she was alone, she slowly got up and made her way to the door, locking it. A glance at her kitchen clock told her that it was 4:00 a.m. She hadn't been out very long, but long enough for him to have gotten far enough away that she doubted the cops would be able to find them. Besides, she hadn't seen him and could only give a vague description of the man's voice and general build.

114

Walking to the sink, she poured some water and took two extra-strength Tylenol; hoping that they would do the trick and that the headache would subside enough for her to be able to function.

Reaching under the sink, she grabbed a pair of latex gloves and then she made her way into the bedroom. Standing on her bed, she reached up into the rafters above her dresser. She had found the hiding place by accident, and had decided that she would put it to good use.

Pulling the small gym bag down, she threw it on the bed, and then replaced the panel she had removed.

Opening her dresser drawer, she took out a pair of black jeans and a t-shirt, then stripped out of her dress and put it in the bag, along with her boots and her jacket. Dressing in her jeans and tee, she threw on a pair of cotton socks and laced up her tennis shoes.

A quick glance through the gym bag confirmed that she had everything else she needed, and then she stepped back into the kitchen to grab her handbag.

There was one more thing she needed to do. Grabbing a disposable cleaning cloth, she quickly wiped the glass she had used and the countertops she had touched, and then she cleaned the outside handle of the door. She knew she hadn't touched anything else, so she was fairly sure that the only prints the police would find would be those of the man who had attacked her. She had been meticulous since she had moved into the apartment and had been careful to leave no trace of herself. Every night before she went to bed, she methodically cleaned her place, ensuring to wipe every counter, door handle, and light switch to ensure there would be no evidence of her existence. These were the steps she believed had been vital for her survival; up until now.

Now, she was once again on the run. Frowning, she looked around the kitchen. She had made slight changes to the room since she had moved in, and it had become a welcome sanctuary for her, but that had come to an abrupt end. Brushing a sudden tear from her cheek, she realized that she never should have let her guard down. She liked James, probably more than she should have, and she had allowed herself to get close to him, and look where it had left her.

Taking one more glance around the room, she double-checked that she hadn't touched anything else. She had wiped every area she had touched before the man had hit her. Hopefully, there would be evidence left that would be enough for James to find and convict the man who had made the threats.

Turning off all the lights, she removed her apartment key from her key chain and wiped it clean. Then she placed it on the table and left without locking up.

She made her way to the small garage on the back part of the lot and found her truck, much as she had left it a few months earlier. Pausing a moment before she started it, she reached in her bag and located her cell phone. Taking a deep breath, she dialed the Marriott.

"Hello?" James answered the phone sounding very groggy, which made Cheri smile.

"Sorry to wake you," she said, and suddenly felt her composure slipping.

James heard it in her voice and was instantly alert. "Cheri? What's wrong?"

Taking a deep breath, she tried to control her emotions. Despite her preparations, she felt her composure slipping. "I had a visitor."

"Cheri, where are you? What happened?"

She ignored his questions. "He wanted me to pass on a message to you."

"Shit!" was James' response.

"He said that you were to back off the Connelly investigation or, and I'm quoting here, 'more than just heads are going to get busted'."

"Cheri? Did they hurt you?"

He heard her voice crack when she made her reply, "I guess mine was the first head to get busted."

"Cheri, where are you?"

"Home," she lied.

"Where do you live? I'm coming over."

"Don't bother, James, I won't be here."

"Cheri? Don't go anywhere. I'll be there as soon as—"

"Damn," he heard her say, "I really liked you," she added as she hung up the phone, knowing that if she kept on the phone, he would persuade her to stay and she couldn't afford to do that. There was too much at stake, too much to lose. Turning off her phone, she started her truck and headed south.

*****

On his way to Cheri's house, James called Bill Koltes, who in turn ordered a rescue squad and a squad car to the scene, and gave strict orders not to use the sirens.

Looking around, he saw a chair had been knocked over and he realized that it was where she had been struck.

"Agent Hogan?"

James turned to find two uniformed officers standing in the doorway.

"I believe Ms. Wood's landlords live in the main house, could you gently wake them and make sure they are alright? Also, see if they heard anything. The perpetrators would have been here about an hour ago."

"Yes sir," was their reply and they headed off toward the house.

Bill Koltes had just arrived as well, along with a complete forensics team.

"Thanks for coming, Bill." James shook his hand. "Damn it, this is my fault."

Bill was surprised by James' outburst. "You and I both know it wasn't."

Bill motioned for James to join him outside as the forensics team got to work. "What do you think?"

James roughly ran his hands through his dark curls. "I don't know. The MO matches that of Connelly. He prides himself on making threats first and then carrying them out if his threats aren't heeded. But how he made my connection with Cheri, I have no idea."

"Well, you have been seen in the young lady's company."

"That's true, and that means I've been under surveillance, and I didn't fucking know it."

Bill put his hand on his friend's shoulder. "Don't beat yourself up. We both know that Connelly's men are trained in covert operations. You wouldn't have seen them even if you had known you were being followed."

"Chief Koltes?" They turned to find one of the officers approaching with an elderly man in tow. "This is Mr. Jenkins. He and his wife own this house and rent the garage apartment to Ms. Wood."

"Is Cheri alright? Was she burglarized?" Mr. Jenkins asked, trying to look past James' shoulder into the apartment.

"We're still trying to determine what happened," Chief Koltes replied. "We do know that something happened sometime between 3:30 and 4:00 a.m. Did you happen to see or hear anything during that time?"

Mr. Jenkins shook his head no. "Unfortunately, Etna and I are both poor of hearing and since we were already in bed, we didn't have our hearing aids in. Etna does remember getting up at about 3:00 a.m. to use the bathroom, but she says she didn't see or hear anything unusual. You can ask her yourself. She's just putting on some coffee."

Against hope, he asked, "Ms. Wood didn't tell you she was leaving?"

"Leaving?" the elderly man frowned.

"Yes, it appears that after she was," James paused to search for the right word that wouldn't alarm the elderly man, "interrupted, she left. Do you have any idea of where she may have gone to?"

Floyd Jenkins shook his head. "No, I have no idea. Maybe Etna will be able to help."

"Thank you, Mr. Jenkins. We appreciate your help," Chief Koltes replied. "Officer, why don't you take Mr. Jenkins back in the house and I'll be in shortly to speak with Mrs. Jenkins."

It had taken her nearly a year of planning. She had promised herself that this time, it would be easier. This time, she had the funds she would need to start over. This time, she'd make the break complete.

Pulling into the parking lot, she grabbed her bags and locked her truck.

The shuttle arrived moments later and she sat back and said a quick prayer that the next phase of her plan would go off without a hitch.

Everything hinged on one aspect—that the passport she was carrying wouldn't be flagged. The fact that it had been issued to her seemed to indicate that it would pass immigration, but if for some reason, it didn't… or if her photo was splashed all over the news…

But she had taken that into consideration six months ago when she had gotten the passport. She had taken care in choosing a new identity that was nothing like her current one. Colored contacts and a new hair color—she hoped they would do the trick.

She had lost some weight since she had her passport photo taken, but she doubted that would be counted against her.

I'll know soon enough, she thought to herself as the shuttle pulled into Portland International Airport.

Luckily, the line for the chartered airline wasn't too long. She was very early, but she knew from experience that these lines were usually packed. True, it wasn't exactly prime tourist season, but all the same, when she turned to see how many people had arrived since she had, she saw that the line was building.

From her bag, she pulled out her printed tickets and her passport and handed them to the airline representative, and then she put her luggage on the scale. She was well under the limit, and her bags were tagged and sent down the conveyor belt. "Gate 47H on the Blue Concourse," the attendant said as she handed back her tickets and her passport.

Cheri thanked the woman and headed for the security checkpoint. *This is it,* she thought.

As she approached the customs desk, she kept repeating her name, reminding herself that to slip up now would be dangerous.

Once again, she handed her passport and tickets to a man sitting behind the desk. She forced a smile to her lips and waited. "Purpose of visit?" she was asked.

"I'm on vacation," she replied. Her belongings were stamped and handed back to her.

"Have a nice trip."

Cheri thanked him and walked through and headed toward her departure gate. Glancing at the clock on the wall, she noticed that she still had two hours to wait until her flight departed at ten a.m. Just enough time, she decided, to grab something to eat and to pick up a few items at the bookstore.

Carrying her McDonald's breakfast and a large coffee to the waiting area, she double-checked that the gate hadn't changed and found that it was still 47H. She settled down in a seat next to the window and as she ate her breakfast, she watched as her plane pulled up to the gate and began the preparations for departure.

She had requested a window seat and as soon as she boarded, she stowed her bag under the seat in front of her and leaned her head back to try to get some sleep. She wasn't out of the woods just yet. Not until the plane landed and she was safely away, would she allow herself to relax her guard.

She did feel better when the plane taxied away from the gate, and when they lifted off, she felt at ease enough to let herself slip off to sleep.

Mexico

She woke to the bump of the wheels touching the tarmac and a glance out the window gave her another sense of relief.

"On behalf of Sun Country Airlines, we'd like to welcome you to Mazatlán, Mexico. We hope you enjoy your stay here and we thank you for choosing Sun Country." As the stewardess began to repeat her message in Spanish, Cheri was glad she had learned the language. While she had been a good student in high school, she had continued her education well into college, and had become relatively proficient in the language.

One more hurdle, she thought; but unless the Feds had notified the Mexican authorities, she doubted that she'd have much trouble. She had been through the Mazatlán Customs before and unless things had changed, she'd be through in no time.

And she was right; the customs officer barely looked at her passport as he stamped one of the empty sheets and handed it back to her. That done, she collected her bag from the carousel and then made her way to the shuttle bus waiting to take her to her hotel.

After the 30-minute journey and another 15 minutes waiting to check in, she was finally shown to her room. Locking the door behind her, she sat her bags down on the floor and sank down on the bed. She'd made it. The last 36 hours seemed a bit of a blur, but she felt confident that she was safe.

She knew that she hadn't been followed from the house; at 4:00 a.m. there hadn't been much traffic and the route she had taken had afforded her the opportunity to watch for any suspicious or familiar cars. As it was, she hadn't even seen another car until about two hours later. By that time, she had hit the Oregon border; she felt sure that the authorities would have been on the lookout for her, and she had taken the time to stop at a motel.

Slipping on her baseball hat first, she had gotten a room on the pretense that she needed to sleep.

Once in the room however, she had quickly bleached her hair and had applied a healthy coat of self-tanning lotion. Half an hour later, she had cut her hair into a shorter bob, being careful to flush the hair down the toilet. Then she had stuffed her hair up into her hat again and left the room, carrying the empty dye containers with her. She wanted to make sure that she left no evidence of her transformation.

Forty-five minutes later, she had arrived at Portland International Airport, where she had thrown the evidence into the garbage, feeling satisfied that no one would make the connection to her. She was not going to assume that the Feds wouldn't find a way to trace her, so she had stuck to her original plan.

Now she was in Mexico, with a new look, a new name and a new life.

She had been thorough in her research, leaving nothing to chance. Her new identity, Anne Manson, hadn't filed an income tax form for over ten years, nor had she made claims on any social security benefits. Her birth date was just a few days after her own, and a search had told her that there were no outstanding warrants or debts in her name. Being from Northern California, it figured that either Ms. Manson was a rebel against the establishment, or she had married young and the system hadn't caught up with her.

The new identity had been borrowed, knowing full well that it would not be damaged in any way. Only if she decided to register for a passport would the truth be known, but by then it wouldn't matter.

Opening her suitcase, she took out her swimsuit and headed for the bathroom. Tomorrow she would be on the move again, but today, she would relax a little and enjoy herself.

*****

She had told the hotel manager that she had received news of a death in the family and that she would have to cut her vacation short. The manager offered her a raincheck on their accommodations, explaining that it wasn't hotel policy to offer refunds; however, they would give her a voucher that would entitle her to return anytime in the next year to stay out the rest of her reservations.

She had accepted the voucher and had caught the shuttle back to the airport. But, instead of heading state-bound, she had waited for the shuttle bus to leave, and then she had hailed a taxi, heading to the center of the city, where she caught a bus to Puerto Vallarta. From there, she took a boat to her final destination—Zihuantanejo.

She had decided long ago that she would settle in the pretty village, thinking that in many ways she was a lot like a character from the movie *The Shawshank Redemption*. While it was true that she had never been accused of murder and had never spent a minute behind bars, like the character, she was on the run, and while she was just an innocent bystander caught in this mess, she knew that she was being pursued, just as the character in the movie had been.

She had prepared for this chapter in her life, not wanting to leave anything to chance. She had been in contact with Inma Hernandez, the elderly woman who owned a small B&B, one she had visited many years ago. In her letters, she had explained that her name was Anne Manson, and she had been a friend of a former guest and had expressed an interest in moving to Mexico, and working at the B&B. The woman was getting on in years, and had mentioned that she often thought about hiring someone to help her run the place.

Over the past year, she had continued to write to Inma, keeping in touch as often as she could. Gradually over the last few months, she had started to write Inma more frequently, firmly establishing herself under her new alias. While she had hoped she wouldn't have to move again, she had recently begun to think it might be time to move on. She was starting to feel settled, and she feared she would start to make mistakes. She had already formed a strong friendship with Inma, so in her last letter to the woman, she had planted the seeds.

She had told Inma that she would like to visit for a week or two, and Inma had been delighted. The sweet woman had even extended an offer to her to stay on longer and move in with her and to help run the place, saying that she longed for an extended vacation in order to visit her family in Southern California. Cheri had told Inma that she would see what she could do, and had promised to visit in August.

When she had to flee Seattle, she had called Inma from a payphone on her way to Portland, telling her that she had lost her job, and asked if her offer was still open. Inma invited her at once and she had agreed to be on the next plane available.

Now, she was on her way to the B&B. After she had gotten off the boat, she had stopped in a small church. She wanted to take a moment to say goodbye to her old life, and to remind herself of who she was now. She prayed that this would be her last journey, and that her past would be left behind her. She prayed for her family, and those she was leaving behind. She also prayed for James Hogan, the handsome FBI agent who she had left in Seattle. She hoped that he wouldn't try to find her, and that he would keep safe and would catch the 'bad guys'.

Taking out her passport, she looked at her photo and at the name now associated with the face. She would no longer go by her former name. She was now Anne Manson.

*****

Walking toward the front door of the B&B, she felt a flutter of nervousness pass through her, as she saw Inma looking through the window. She smiled and waved her acknowledgement.

"Anne!" Inma Hernandez sounded excited to see her. "I am very happy you are here! Did you have a good flight?"

Anne smiled and felt herself relax a little more. "Yes, I did; and thank you again for this opportunity."

The older woman waved her off. "Nonsense, you are helping me out; and besides, you're like family. Enough about that; this week you are my guest, nothing more. I don't have anyone staying at the moment—I usually close down for a few months in the summer, but now that you are here… but we'll talk about that later. Are you hungry? You must be tired. Would you like to rest a bit?"

Inma was rattling on and Anne couldn't help but smile. Giving her a big hug, she said, "It is good to be here."

Inma finally realized that she had been talking non-stop and laughed at herself. "Let me show you to your room, and then meet me out on the terrace. We can have some lunch and then I'll tell you the wonderful news."

Anne looked questioning, but Inma wasn't about to ruin the surprise. "No, do as I say, get settled and then we'll talk." Then she gave the younger woman another hug. "Here is your room," she said, opening a door on the second floor. The room was beautiful. It was a large room with a sitting area that had a love seat and a square white table with a lamp and a stack of hard cover books. Then there were a few steps that led up to the main bedroom, which had a large four poster bed, a large round night side table and a high back rocking chair.

To her left, there was an antique wardrobe against the wall, and next to it was the door that led to a large bathroom. The bathroom was furnished with a clawfoot bathtub and a separate shower.

Next to the bed, there was a set of glass doors that lead out to a small balcony that faced the ocean. The view was spectacular.

Anne knew that this was one of Inma's best rooms and she thanked her for the use of it. Waved off again, Inma left her to unpack.

Opening the wardrobe, she saw that Inma had made some renovations, adding 5 drawers on one side, giving her plenty of room for all her belongings.

Changing into a sundress, she went to meet the woman. She found Inma sitting under a large sun umbrella, sipping a beer. "Cold one?"

Anne nodded. "Sure."

Reaching into the cooler next to her, Inma grabbed a Dos XXs beer and handed it to Anne. "Welcome to Mexico." Inma raised her beer to Anne and they clinked their bottles together.

"So, what's the news?"

Inma smiled. "My sister has invited me to come stay with her next month."

"That's wonderful!" Anne smiled back at her.

"So that means I'll be leaving you in charge; if that's ok with you."

"Of course, it is; that's why I'm here, right?" was Anne's confident reply. Sitting back against the wicker chair, Anne looked out at the ocean. "It is so beautiful here." Inma smiled in agreement.

The women sat in silence for a few moments and then Inma stirred. "Now, I don't want you feeling that you need to spend all your time with this old lady. I expect that you have some things you will want to do."

Anne smiled. "What old lady?"

Inma smiled back. "You are a sweet girl."

Anne continued, "I would like to do some tourist stuff. That way I'll be more useful to your guests; and it would be a good start learning the places the locals go, stuff like that."

"That's a good idea. I'd like to suggest that this first week you concentrate on having fun. I'll start showing you where I do the shopping and things like that; introduce you to the merchants so they won't give you the tourist prices. Next week, I'll start showing you the ropes. As I mentioned, I'm planning to head off on my holiday next month, so we have plenty of time to get you organized."

"Thanks, Inma. The same goes for you. I don't want you to feel like you have to entertain me. After all, I'm here to do a job, and besides, I'm sure there is a lot you need to get done before you take your vacation."

Inma nodded. "There are some things, and if you wouldn't mind, maybe you could help me with some of them."

"Of course, I'd be happy to help you. What do you need?"

"Well, I need to do a little shopping, and I thought I'd take the bus into Mexico City. But if you don't mind driving, I have my nephew's jeep here; he wants me to sell it, but I haven't gotten around to doing that yet, and you can use it until I do."

"Sounds fun, shall we go tomorrow?" Anne offered.

"No, we can wait until next week. You are on vacation this week. But perhaps next Tuesday, if that's ok with you?"

"Are you sure?"

"Yes. Now, I want you to sit back and relax. I'll go get the tourist brochures I have and you can start planning your week."

While Inma went to get the brochures, Anne sat back and thought of the handsome FBI agent. She had meant it when she had said she liked him. She had felt a connection with him. A dangerous connection—one that, had those goons not forced her to leave, she might have been in real danger of getting in over her head.

Taking a sip of her beer, she told herself that this was for the best. She wouldn't have wanted to deceive him, but she wouldn't have had the flexibility to be completely honest with him either. If he learned about her past… but she didn't even want to think about that. Now, she just wanted to relax and enjoy the start of her new life.

*****

Anne spent the rest of the week going on every tourist tour or activity she could find; making notes on which ones were worth their value and which should be missed.

By the end of the week, she felt as if she had been going non-stop and was ready to relax into her new role.

The next Tuesday, Anne and Inma set off for Mexico City. Inma's nephew's jeep was only a few years old and in great condition. When Anne asked why he wanted to sell it, Inma explained that he had moved to California with his new wife and their baby daughter, and they had decided to get a larger SUV instead.

As Inma directed her, Anne did a quick calculation and then asked Inma how much he wanted for the jeep. "He's asking 100,000 pesos, but I know he'll take 70,000," was her answer.

"Would it be ok if I bought it?" Anne asked.

Inma seemed surprised. "Are you sure you want to spend your savings?"

"I put some money aside for a car, and this is much nicer than I would have expected to find. But if you feel uncomfortable selling it to me, I'd understand."

Inma patted her hand. "Not at all; I just don't want you spending all your savings."

"No, this was money specifically earmarked for a car. That is, if you're sure he'll take $4,000 in US dollars for it. Otherwise, I'll have to wait a couple of months to save up the difference."

"No, he'll take the $4,000. He'll be happy to get it in US dollars, and not in pesos. When we are in town, we can get the paperwork completed with my lawyer and then the jeep will be yours for the drive home."

"I'll need to get car insurance," Anne added, but Inma dismissed her with a wave of her hand. "It will all be taken care of," and then she changed the subject, reminding Anne that the Mexican way of life and way of doing business was definitely different than in the States.

The drive to the coastal town of Lázaro Cárdenas took about an hour and a half and they headed for Inma's attorney first, where they signed the vehicle transfer forms, and Inma arranged to wire the funds to her nephew.

Anne would wire the $4,000 into Inma's account via the internet later when they got back from their shopping trip. Then Anne waited in the reception area as Inma spoke with the attorney on other personal business.

Emerging from the office, Anne overheard Inma's attorney saying, "I'll have the paperwork ready for your signatures next week. In the meantime, if there's anything else you want to include, just call my assistant and she'll add it to the paperwork."

"Thank you, Eric." Inma shook the man's hand and then the two women were off to buy Inma a few new outfits for her journey.

Anne also picked up a few items for herself. During her excursions the previous week, she had discovered that she would need a few more swimming suits if she was going to enjoy the various water sports that the island offered.

Another swimming suit and a couple pairs of board shorts were definitely in order, as well as a good pair of water shoes.

Anne had already learned that the prices at the local beach shop were definitely inflated and so Inma took her to a small shop the locals used.

On the drive home, Inma took Anne a different direction, which took them past Inma's favorite restaurant, and they stopped for dinner. Once they had ordered, Inma explained that the restaurant was where her late husband had proposed to her, 40 years ago. "Now, I come here whenever I get the chance. I will miss it when I am gone, but there are other places I will enjoy seeing again."

Anne thought of the restaurant on the ocean where she had taken James. She hoped that one day she'd be able to return there, but she doubted it. She would just have to find another secluded diamond in the rough here in Mexico.

*****

During the following two weeks, the Casa had quite a few guests, which gave Anne the chance to learn the way Inma ran the B&B. The meals were easy to make, some huevos rancheros, sausages, cut fruit, toast, scrambled eggs and homemade coffee cake. Every morning, Anne and Inma would get up at 7 a.m. to get the breakfast ready. Breakfast was served between 8:30 and 10 a.m. The kitchen was open to the dining area, so it gave them the chance to see their guests arrive, and Anne would approach them with the offer of coffee or tea. A long table was set with the ready-made breakfast options.

Anne would also take their special orders and then she prepared the orders. Inma, meanwhile, was busy relaxing. Anne had insisted that Inma let her run the shop, under her supervision, saying that then they would both know if she would be ready to handle it on her own.

Anne made a few suggestions to add to the menu and a few other suggestions, which Inma like and implemented. By the end of the second week, they were both confident that Anne would be fine running the place on her own.

The week before Inma was due to leave on her trip; she closed the B&B and told Anne not to accept any reservations for the next two weeks.

Because the majority of the guests were regulars—guests who returned every year or two—it was easy to accommodate her request.

On Sunday, after they had finished cleaning up after the last of the guests, Inma had invited Anne to join her on the terrace. Changing into one of her new sundresses, Anne found Inma sitting with a glass of ice water. Anne noticed that she had also changed into a fresh dress.

Upon seeing Anne approach, the older woman suddenly sat up, and as if something came to her mind, she said, "Let's have some champagne."

Anne laughed. "Why not!"

Anne helped Inma get the bottle from the wine cooler, as Inma grabbed a couple of champagne glasses. Carefully opening the bottle, Anne poured the champagne, and then Inma raised her glass to Anne, saying, "To new beginnings." Anne smiled and clinked Inma's glass and was taking a sip of her champagne when Inma added, "And to the new manager and owner of the Casa."

Nearly spitting out the liquid, she coughed, "What?"

"The job's yours," Inma gestured to the property, "that is, if you want it?"

Anne was speechless. She knew that Inma was getting on in years, and that running the place was beginning to take its toll on her, but Anne hadn't expected her to want to sell it. Anne didn't know what to say; while she had put plenty of money aside to live on, she knew she couldn't afford to buy the place outright.

Inma must have read her mind. "Anne, don't worry. It is all set. I have made up a will and named you as the manager and co-owner of the Casa. I own the Casa outright, so there will be no expenses other than general running costs." Steering Anne back to her chair, she added, "Now, I don't plan on leaving this earth anytime soon, but I am tired of looking after the place. I want to travel and see my family. I want to see the world. A number of years ago, I established a trust fund, it basically pays for everything, including a healthy salary for you."

Seeing that Anne was about to object, she held up her hand and continued, "No, I won't hear any objections, unless you don't want the job. I made up my mind long ago that when you finally came to visit, I would tell you my plan to make you the manager of the Casa. You know that I don't have any children;

Mr. Hernandez and I were not blessed with any, and you have always been so kind, remembering my birthday, holidays…it's meant a lot to me. Making you co-owner ensures that you can make most decisions about the Casa on your own, without having to consult me first. My attorney can explain it much better than I can."

"You're my friend," Anne replied.

"And you are mine. That's why I know you are the right person to carry on running the Casa in my absence."

Anne didn't know what to say. She suddenly felt guilty for deceiving the elderly woman, but she knew that she couldn't afford to come clean. Telling Inma the truth of who she was wouldn't only put her life in danger, but it would put Inma's life in danger as well.

Inma reached out and patted Anne's hand. "Don't give me your answer today. Let us just enjoy the day. I've arranged a meeting with my attorney on Monday. We'll make everything final then. Alright?"

Anne stood up and went to Inma, giving her a heartfelt hug. "I really don't know what to say. You know that I love this place, but I never, for one moment, thought about anything like this."

Inma hugged her back and then wiping a tear from her cheek said, "You have just made me a very happy old woman."

"Hey, who you calling old?" Anne wiped a tear from her own cheek.

"Enough about that. I've some fresh shrimp and lobster in the sink for our dinner, and later I thought we could go down to the village and I'll introduce you to a few old friends."

*****

Monday morning, Anne drove Inma into Mexico City and once again, she found herself seated in front of Eric Santana. The portly gentleman smiled at Inma and said, "So, you've finally told the young lady your plan." Then he turned toward Anne. "I must agree, you seem to have chosen a very competent business partner. You'll want to read everything carefully," he added as he handed a large document to Anne and another to Inma.

Anne read the first line and looked up at the attorney and then at Inma. She began to stand, to leave, but Inma laid her hand on her arm, urging her to remain seated. Looking down at the document again, she stared at her name staring back at her. Her birth name.

"I'm sorry to have startled you, my dear," the older woman said.

"It's my fault really," Mr. Santana explained. "When Inma told me that she wanted to leave everything to you, I insisted that we do a background check."

Inma interrupted him, "I remembered who you were from your first visit, all those years ago," she said with a reassuring pat on Anne's hand. "When Eric did his research, he told me that he had discovered that you were somehow mixed up with some very bad people and presumed dead. It was then that we decided to keep things to ourselves, to protect you. When you arrived, I knew instantly that it really was you," she added with a smile.

"But since I need to make this all legal," Eric continued, "we had to put your legal name on some of the paperwork. Do not worry, only your current name will be used on the paperwork that will be registered with the courts. It's a nice legal loophole that allows us to do it this way, and because everything is being handled by Inma's trust fund, no one will ever find the paper trail that could cause you trouble."

Anne stared again at the paper in front of her. "How long have you known?" she asked.

Eric answered her question, "Over a year. I suspected it about the time you started writing again."

Taking her hand, Inma explained, "You and I had become friends from the beginning, and when you stopped writing for a while, I assumed you had just gotten busy with life. Then when you started writing again, well, I assumed that the name change was that you had gotten married, or divorced. But I decided not to ask you about it."

Eric could read the fear on her face. "You have nothing to worry about. Your true name was never mentioned and never in connection with your other names. Only Inma and I know of your past. No one else will ever know. You have my word on that."

Anne thought about it for a moment and realized that if they were going to turn her in, then they would have done so a year ago.

"Anne," Inma squeezed Anne's hand between her own, "you are safe here. But I did want you to know that I knew who you used to be. I didn't want you feeling that you were keeping something from me. I know you've been wrestling with that, and now you can set your mind at ease."

Anne brushed the tear from her cheek. So much had happened over the last 24 hours, and she felt overwhelmed. "So, will you still accept my offer?"

Anne gave Inma a hug and laughed. "Yes, I'd be honored."

Eric smiled and handed both women some tissues. "I'm glad we got that out of the way. Now, if you will both carefully read the documents, we have quite a few items to go over."

An hour and a half later, Inma and Anne were on their way back to the B&B. Anne's head was still swimming, and when they got home, Inma suggested she go for a walk on the beach to clear her head. Anne agreed, with a promise to return in the hour. Inma had arranged for a celebration meal with a few of her friends and she insisted that Anne join them. "After all, you are the reason I'm celebrating," Inma insisted.

For the first half hour, Anne's mind was racing. She was now the co-owner of a successful B&B, with a guaranteed salary that would insure her the luxury of a quiet season if need be. That, and Inma knew who she was, who she really was. She knew about her past and she still hadn't balked at the idea of leaving her pride and joy to her.

Anne made a silent vow that she would never let Inma down, and spent the next half hour thinking about ways to increase the profitability of the B&B.

Inma had insisted that Anne make any changes she wanted, including expanding the house if she thought it made sense, but Anne didn't think that would be necessary. There were a few small changes she'd like to make, mostly ecstatic changes that wouldn't cost that much, but that should pay for themselves in the long run.

It was coming close to the end of the peak season, so Anne would have plenty of time to make the changes before the next season. She would run them by Inma first, but she felt sure Inma would approve.

Stopping to look out over the ocean, Anne shook her head in disbelief. So much had happened, and finally it looked like things were starting to settle down for her. When she had moved to Seattle, she had always known that it would be a temporary situation; somehow, she knew that her past would catch up with her and that she'd be forced to flee again. When the goons had visited her, she had felt that it would be better to leave than to press her luck. Publicity, after all, was something she did not need.

Who would have thought that coming to Mexico would be the place where her past would catch up with her, but with unexpected results? Instead of having to flee again, she was being given the opportunity to finally put her past behind her and have a fresh start, and all thanks to a lovely lady who seemed more like the grandmother Anne never knew, than a causal acquaintance.

She realized that she would miss her over the next few months, and started walking again, heading back toward the B&B. She wanted to spend as much time with her as possible before she left on Friday for her holiday.

*****

Inma had arranged for everyone to meet at her favorite restaurant at 7 p.m. and had insisted that they take a taxi so they could 'party', as she put it.

Inma had bought a new dress for the occasion, and Anne pulled out the black dress she had worn at the book signing party. She decided to remove the detachable ruby string on the back, as she doubted the night would warrant such a fancy dress and she didn't want to outshine Inma. Then, pulling the dress over her head, she realized that she had lost a few pounds in the month since she had last worn it, and she was happy with the results. Clipping a silk flower into her hair, she grabbed a colorful wrap and went in search of Inma.

She found Inma standing in front of the hallway mirror, trying to connect the clasp of her necklace. "Here, let me help you."

Inma handed the beautiful necklace to Anne and waited while she clasped the delicate piece of jewelry. "Thank you, Anne." Then turning, Inma added, "You look beautiful."

"Thank you, you're looking pretty fetching yourself. Are you sure you're not meeting some young man tonight?" Anne teased her friend.

Inma winked at her. "Well, you'd never know who you'll meet, and we women must always be prepared."

Anne linked arms with her friend and steered her toward the door and the waiting taxi. "Let's go see what we can find." Inma laughed and allowed herself to be led to the door.

The restaurant had prepared a special menu in Inma's honor, stating that they were losing one of their favorite customers. Anne thought they were being a little dramatic. After all, Inma was to be gone only four months, but she went along with the festive atmosphere.

Inma had invited ten other guests; many of the people Anne had met the weeks since she had been in Mexico, some were new to Anne, but they all greeted her as if she were Inma's long-lost daughter.

After the plates were cleared away, the waiters made sure that everyone's glasses were filled. Inma stood up and proposed a toast. "My friends, I want to thank you all for coming tonight to see me off. As you all know, I leave on Friday for California to visit my sister and her family, and as you know, I will be leaving the Casa in Anne's capable hands. I expect you all to check in with her to see if there's anything she needs.

"Also, as most of you know, I've wanted to be near my sister for a while now and I am looking forward to finally being able to spend the time traveling with her. What I haven't told you is that I have received permission to stay in California as long as I wish, and it is my plan to do so."

There was a round of applause, and then she continued, "My sister has fixed up her garage into an apartment for me, and you are all welcome to visit anytime."

It was at this point that Anne began to realize that Inma wasn't planning on returning. A glance around the room confirmed her suspicions. These people weren't there to wish their friend 'Bon Voyage'; they were there to say 'Goodbye'.

Inma's next words confirmed her suspicions. "I want you all to know that I consider each of you as close friends, as family, and I will miss you all, but I've always said that if given the opportunity, that I would immigrate to the United States, and now that I've been given the opportunity, I'm not going to hesitate."

Swallowing back her tears, Anne stood and proposed a toast, "To our friend, Inma, and to the next chapter in her life. She is the youngest and the most adventurous woman I know."

Anne gave her a hug around the shoulders and then stepped back as the others approached to give Inma a hug.

Anne snuck away to the ladies' room, where she tried to get a hold of her emotions.

"Anne?" Inma was standing at the door. "Are you alright?" the elderly woman asked as she stepped toward Anne. Anne nodded, not trusting her voice. "I'm sorry I keep springing these surprises on you." Inma gave her hug. "But I couldn't exactly land all the news on you at once," she added with a wink.

Anne hugged her again. "I know. I'm just trying to take it all in."

"You'll have plenty of time for that once you have the place to yourself. You have never seemed to me to be one not to meet a challenge head-on, but believe me, this is an easy challenge," she added with a wink. "Besides, nothing has really changed, you are still here to live and work. The only difference is that you won't need to get three or four jobs to make ends meet. You'll be working for yourself and that's my gift to you."

"I just don't want people to think I'm taking advantage of you." Anne stepped back as she brushed the tears from her face.

"Honey, they've all known that I planned to leave the place in your capable hands. You were just the last person I told." She smiled sheepishly. Again, Anne was left feeling shocked.

"I'm old, Anne, but I'm not senile. I knew that people would draw the wrong conclusions if I left my plan a secret until the end, so I've been telling them about you for years; always telling them that you would be taking over the Casa when I got too old to do it myself. Most of them believe you are a distant relative, and to be honest, I have never corrected them. You're like the daughter I never had and if you were a little younger, I might have even adopted you," she added with a smile.

"Now, are you ready to get back to the others? I've ordered some champagne and I want to make sure you and I get a glass or two," she added as she gave Anne another hug.

"Yes, I'm ok. Thank you, Inma, you are a very special woman and I consider you much more than just a friend."

"Enough of that," Inma said as she linked arms with her, "or you'll have me crying."

On that note, the ladies joined the others and the rest of the evening was filled with laughter and song.

*****

On Friday, Anne saw Inma off at the airport. She had packed all her personal belongings in three large suitcases, having already sent the rest of her things by freight during the week. Everything else that was left at the Casa was part of the B&B and was considered part of the business assets, so if there was a fire, a burglary or a hurricane, everything would be replaced with the insurance money.

After Anne watched Inma's plane take off, she slowly made her way back to the jeep. She didn't feel like going directly back to the empty house, so she dragged out her map and plotted a different route back. Inma had told her about a lovely mountain view and she decided to make that her destination. Two hours later, Anne was standing on the backseat of her jeep, looking out over a beautiful mountain range that seemed to stretch out as far as the eye could see.

Taking out her camera, she began to shoot a panoramic photo. With luck, the photos would do the place justice. If so, then she placed to put them together in a large frame and send it to Inma as a friendly reminder of the country she had left behind. Then she thought that she should get a similar shot of the ocean view from the terrace at the B&B. The two composites would make a nice compliment to each other. Finishing the shot, Anne sat back down and drove back to the Casa.

It was nearly five o'clock by the time she got back and she made herself a bean and cheese enchilada for dinner and sat on the terrace sipping a Dos XXs.

The house was quiet and, for the first time that day, Anne let herself think about her situation. This was her home now. Inma had left everything to her. Now she had a house, a business and a well-established trust fund to live on.

Financially, she would not have to worry about anything for quite a while, and living in a small town in Mexico gave her the peace of mind that she would be safe—that no one would ever make the connection to her past. Thanks to Inma and her attorney, even her identity would remain safe. This was the first time in a long time that Anne would finally allow herself to relax.

Looking out at the ocean, she thought back to all the events that had shaped her life, and that had brought her to this day.

Four years ago, when she had first visited the Casa, she had been on vacation with two girlfriends she knew from college. She had fallen in love with the place instantly and had promised herself that she would return. She had struck up a friendship with Inma immediately and had promised to keep in touch, which she had, by sending birthday cards, Christmas cards and an occasional letter.

Then her life had taken that dramatic turn and she had fled, hoping that the men after her would never find her. It wasn't that what she had done was exactly criminal; although she wasn't sure the police would take the same view. But she had acted on instinct and right or wrong she hadn't turned back.

Once she had arrived in Seattle, she had started writing Inma again as Anna, and had continued their friendship, albeit under a new identify.

She had hoped that it was all safely behind her, but then the handsome FBI agent had shown up and her life was once again thrown into chaos.

Coming to Mexico had always been her last-ditch escape route, and when she had been forced to use it, she had felt that if it didn't work, then there would be nowhere else she would be able to go.

Getting past the immigration officers in both the States and in Mexico had given her some confidence. Then when Inma had told her that she was her heir, and that they knew of her past, she realized that if anyone else had made the connection, they would have already tracked her down; which meant that she was safe.

Finishing her beer, she took her dishes back into the kitchen and cleaned up her mess. Then she grabbed a pad of paper and a pen, a fresh beer and sat down again to map out her plans. Tomorrow, her new life would begin in full swing... Again.

Chicago

James picked up the thick file and handed it to the district attorney. "The evidence is all in the file, Matt; all you have to do is to present it."

Matt Johnson smiled as he took the folder from him. "Another slam-dunk, huh?"

"We can only hope," was James' reply. It had been nearly two years of hard work, and despite the challenges, he felt confident that he had finally gathered enough evidence for a conviction. This time, he felt sure that they had him.

Matt looked down at the name on the front of the folder—Connelly. "It would be good to nail this one to the floor." Then, as he headed toward the door he added, "See you in court."

James waited until he was alone then he picked up his phone and called his superior. "Chief, the file has just been handed off to the DA. I suspect that the case will be heard on Friday. If all goes well, I'd like to take an extended leave of absence."

"You're going to try to find her, aren't you?" James didn't answer, confirming his boss' suspicions. "Well, you've certainly earned a long vacation. How long will you need?"

"I'm not sure. A month, maybe two?" was his answer.

"Take two, but I want to be kept in the loop if you need any of our resources." Then he had to ask, "Do you have any leads?"

"A few but none that look very promising," James admitted.

"I wish you luck. I know you've already put a lot of hours into this one." Then as a word of caution, he added, "But remember, we still haven't found all the bodies that Connelly buried. She just may end up being another of his victims."

James frowned into the phone and said goodbye to his superior.

He knew that it was a possibility that his chief was right. Connelly didn't like loose ends, and she was definitely a loose end. That is, if she was still alive. But something told him that Cheri was still alive, and he planned on finding her.

His friend George thought that James was just being optimistic. That it was nearly impossible for someone to plan their own disappearance, let alone to plan one in the space of an hour, but James just couldn't let it go. The fact that there were no fingerprints belonging to the young lady found at her apartment, told a bigger story than James could simply ignore. Maybe it was her parting words that were still haunting him or perhaps it was the fact that he was the cause of getting her hurt, and possibly even killed, that wasn't sitting right—but whatever it was, James was going to track down every lead—no matter how remote it may seem.

The ringing of his phone drew him back to the present.

"Hogan."

"Judge Webber is sitting the case," Matt Johnson announced, "and he wants the pre-trial to begin tomorrow morning at 9:00 a.m. sharp."

"He's not taking any chances, is he?" James stated the obvious. "Well, at least we know that Webber isn't corrupt. I'll see you tomorrow. Oh, and tell the judge that he will be given police protection."

"I already did," Matt replied before hanging up.

James dialed his boss again and relayed the good news and then he went to work clearing off his open cases; reassigning them and preparing for his time off. With Judge Webber overseeing the case, it would be a quick trial. Webber was as committed to the program as James was and he didn't tolerate delays or any other nonsense in his court room. The defense team would try to stall, but the judge wouldn't allow it.

James predicted that he would be off to Seattle by the weekend.

*****

The next day, Connelly was arraigned and held without bail. He would sit in jail until he went to trial. The judge hadn't offered any bail, knowing that the crime boss could easily arrange for bail no matter the amount, and he was far too dangerous to let out. The trial date had been set for two months' time, which still gave James the time to search for Cheri. In the meantime, his team had been instructed to increase their efforts in finding the five missing victims. If any of them were still alive, then he wanted them found and put somewhere safe where Connelly's men couldn't get to them.

Seattle

It had been nearly a month and James was still no closer to finding her. Looking back over his notes, he started to wonder if he was going at this the right way; perhaps he needed to switch directions.

So far, he had been concentrating on the assumption that Cheri had gone to a friend's place to stay and he had been busy asking everyone who knew her in Seattle for some kind of information that would lead him to find her.

Then he had focused his efforts of trying to track down her past, but it seemed that prior to turning up in Seattle well over a year ago, the woman didn't seem to exist. She had told everyone that she was from Nebraska, but when he had checked the state records, no one by that name had ever been born, much less lived in the state; which meant that she had been a runaway and had used a fake name.

In fact, she had applied for her social security number only after she had moved to Seattle. The birth certificate she had produced had been a fake too. James discovered that it had originally belonged to a Charlotte Wood, who had passed away ten years earlier in a car crash in Connecticut.

James then focused his search on any missing woman that vaguely fit her general appearance, but once again, he struck out. He followed a few leads and managed to reunite one young lady with her estranged parents, but nothing else.

What next? He asked himself. He was running out of options and out of time. The Connelly trial was only a month away and he knew that he would be called back to testify.

He thought back over the length of the investigation, to a possible connection. Looking at her photo again, he couldn't help but think that perhaps the reason she had been targeted had been because of the leak. The leak that had led to the death of a good agent and a personal friend of his, and possibly to Cheri's death as well.

Looking more closely at the picture, he suddenly had a thought. It was a long shot but… Picking up his mobile phone, he called Jimmy Smith, Seattle's top forensic artist. "Jimmy, do you have some time to do a mock-up for me?"

"Sure, but I thought you were on vacation."

"I am, but it's kind of a working holiday. I'm staying at the Hilton. Could I buy you a beer and show you what I got?"

"You know me; I never turn down a free beer. How does seven tonight sound?"

"I'll meet you at O'Shea's."

"Great, then I'll have a Jamison *and* a Guinness." He laughed and hung up.

*****

Jimmy looked at the two photos and then he looked back up at James. "It's a long shot, but let me play around here for a moment."

The differences between the two photographs were obvious, but there was something about the smile. It had given James the idea in the first place.

Taking his phone out of his pocket, he took a snapshot of each of the photos and then emailed them to his work address. Then he pulled out his laptop and began working with one of his programs.

James ordered another round of beers, sat back, and waited while Jimmy worked his magic.

The frown on Jimmy's brow concerned James. *Damn!* James watched as his last hope seemed to vanish. If Jimmy couldn't see the connection, then James didn't know where he'd go next.

"Well, tell me what you think," Jimmy said, looking over the two images he had created. "I took each photo and made adjustments, that way I couldn't bias my results." Then he pushed his laptop in front of James.

Leaning over, he studied the two images. "Damn," he spoke aloud this time.

"Looks like you were right. It's the same woman. Question is, what are you going to do now?"

James looked up at Jimmy and shook his head. "I have no idea."

Seeing the waitress approaching, James closed the laptop. "Jimmy, I'd appreciate it if you could keep this under your hat."

"Yeah, that's probably a good idea," Jimmy agreed. "But it still doesn't mean that she got away twice."

"I know, but at least I can run with this theory, and if I still come up empty-handed, at least I'll know I tried everything."

Jimmy nodded. "Tread lightly though. If anyone gets an idea of what you are up to—"

"I know," James interrupted him, "she'll be dead for sure."

Three Months Later
Mexico

Anne smiled as she said goodbye to the last of her guests. The Casa had had a successful initial run under her ownership, and she was pleased to know that several of her guests had already pre-booked for the next season. However, while the Casa had previously been booked for the following week, the hurricane warnings had caused her guests to back out. She couldn't blame them. Hurricane Danny had already laid waste to a good portion of the Caribbean, and while it showed signs of slowing down, they expected it to hit the Mexican coast within the week. Anne had already begun making preparations. Inma had even called to give her some last-minute instructions. The older woman had survived two previous hurricanes and Anne was thankful for her suggestions, which included heading into the mountains to wait out the storm.

Inma had told her about a small home she and her husband had built, which Inma had retained. It was her intention to return there when she was 'old and gray' to live out the final days of her life. In the meantime, she had kept it stocked and ready for emergency conditions such as this. "I was there the week before you arrived, so I know it's still in one piece," she assured Anne.

Anne wanted to head there when the weather started to get worse. She didn't want to leave the Casa unattended in case the storm missed them. Meanwhile, she planned on battening down the hatches and making the place as stormproof as she could.

*****

Two days later, the storm was fast approaching and Anne was busy making her final preparations when she heard a knock on the front door. She was in the process of carrying a box of canned goods out to the jeep in the back of the house, so she called out, "Come in, I'll be right with you."

Setting the box into the back of the jeep, she turned to find her neighbor, Stephano. "Senorita Anne, why are you still here? They say everyone should be heading away."

Anne smiled. "I'm just grabbing a few last items and then I'm off. Why are you still here?"

"We were just leaving when we saw your door open," was his reply.

Anne nodded. "Thank you for checking in on me. I appreciate it. Not to worry, I'll be out of here in fifteen minutes. Be safe and I'll see you when this all blows over."

"Gracias, hasta luego." The older gentleman waved goodbye and pulled away.

Walking back into the B&B, Anne double-checked all the windows and verified that everything was unplugged. She had already turned off the main circuit breaker, but she tried the lights to make sure. She locked the front door, and as she was pulling down the shutters, she felt someone behind her.

"Hello Cheri."

Turning, she found herself looking down the stairs at FBI Agent James Hogan. A gust of wind reminded her of the approaching storm and she turned and bent down to finish locking down the shutter.

Over her shoulder, she found herself shouting over the growing storm, "We're about to get hit by the hurricane. I suggest you get back in your car and get to safety." Standing up, she turned again to find him striding up the stairs toward her.

"I'm not going anywhere without you."

The rain started to come down harder and she asked, "Where is your car?"

"The taxi driver dropped me off and left."

Cursing, she pointed toward her jeep. "Get in, we have to get out of here."

James threw his bag in the back seat of the jeep and got into the passenger side as she got in behind the wheel. Backing the car out of the drive, she headed inland toward Inma's mountain retreat.

"Cheri," James began to talk, but she interrupted him, "No, not yet." Then she turned her head and looked at him. "Please?"

James nodded in agreement and they drove in silence. Not that they could have had a conversation. The wind and rain were full force now and the sound of hail was almost deafening on top of the jeep. She was happy she had put the hard cover on; otherwise, she was sure the soft cover would have been torn to bits.

The driving was treacherous, as she found herself swerving to miss several fallen trees and other debris. A couple of hours later, she finally reached the house.

She had made several trips to the house over the last few days, delivering her clothing and other supplies, so she knew the directions well. All the same, it took them longer than expected and it was getting dark by the time they reached the place.

"I'll get the door," she shouted over the noise of the storm, and she jumped out of the jeep and ran up to the door.

Unlocking the door, she stepped in and switched on the light. Thankfully, the generator was behaving itself. She turned and found James standing behind her with his bag and the box of supplies in his arms. "Thank you," she said, "go ahead and put that box on the table." Then she stepped past him and back out into the pouring rain. He heard the jeep start up again, and he quickly set the box on the table and ran to stop her from leaving. But to his surprise, he found her backing the jeep into a covered carport.

He waited on the porch for her and when she ran up to the house, she slowed down as she saw him. Stopping in front of him, she studied his face for a moment, trying to gauge his mood, then she walked past him and back into the cabin.

Following her in, he watched as she kicked off her wet sneakers and then the lights flickered as they heard a loud clap of thunder. Walking to the table, she grabbed a match and lit the lantern that was sitting on the table. Looking back at James, she noted his wet clothes. "We should get out of these wet clothes. The bathroom is the first door down that hall," she told him and then she walked down the hall and disappeared in the bedroom.

Stepping out of his wet shoes, he left them next to hers and then grabbed his bag and headed for the bathroom. Stopping outside the room, he stared at the closed bedroom door where she had gone, and then he went into the bathroom and changed out of his wet things.

She hurried and changed out of her wet clothes, carefully hanging them up to dry, and slipped into a dry pair of jeans and a fresh t-shirt. Slipping on some cotton socks, she stepped into her second pair of tennis shoes and grabbed her Mexican poncho. The temperature was already dropping, so she went back into the main room and began to light a fire.

The storm outside picked up in velocity and the house seemed to shake against the wind. Again, she instinctively looked up at the ceiling, expecting the roof to suddenly blow off.

"Did they say when the hurricane would hit land?"

She looked over at James, who was standing in the hallway, also looking up at the ceiling. He too had changed into jeans and t-shirt. "Not until tomorrow. This is just the pre-storm. But don't worry, Inma told me that we are too far up in the mountains for any flood risks. It's just the wind we have to worry about," she replied, and then went back to work building a fire in the stone fireplace.

"I wouldn't have recognized you," he whispered.

She paused in her preparations a moment, but didn't comment on his remark. Continuing with her task, she hoped that he would drop the subject. She wasn't ready yet.

"Hell, I didn't recognize you when we met in Seattle." Now she could hear the frustration in his voice.

She stopped again, and watched to see if her efforts would take off. Picking up some kindling, she added it to the fire and once she was satisfied that it would catch, she sat back and stared into the growing fire.

"I'm sorry I had to leave that way," she finally said. "I'm sorry for any trouble I may have caused you."

She heard him approach and felt him squat down beside her, but she didn't turn to look at him. She didn't trust her emotions and she didn't want to break down in front of him.

James too was fighting his emotions. He wasn't sure if he wanted to hug her or throttle her. "Why didn't you tell me who you were when I met you in Seattle?" He finally asked.

She glanced back at him, finally realizing that he knew her true identity.

"For the same reason I couldn't tell you who I was when I called you in Chicago. If anyone knew I was still alive..." she left it at that; he knew the consequences as well as she did.

*****

He was waiting for her to open up. She knew it too, but she wasn't going to talk, not tonight, and she thought it only fair to warn him. She turned toward him. "I know you want some answers, but I'm not going to get into it tonight." She tried to read his expression. "It's going to take a lot of alcohol for me to open up, and I don't feel like dealing with a hangover tomorrow."

But he was still going to press her for some answers tonight. She could read it in his eyes. Laying her hand over his, she squeezed his hand. "Please James, leave it be; just for tonight."

He could see the fear in her eyes and he relented. Turning his hand under her, he gently squeezed back. "Ok, I won't push. But I will need some answers."

She nodded "I know, and you deserve them."

"Thank you." He nodded. Then he asked the one question he couldn't wait on. "I do have one question I need to ask."

Anne took an unsteady breath and waited.

"What should I call you?"

She smiled at that. "Anne. Anne is who I am now."

Puzzled, he shrugged. "Ok, Anne it is." Then he forced himself to change the subject. Looking around the cabin, he asked, "How did you find this place?"

"It's Inma's retirement home. She told me to use it when the weather got bad. She stayed here during the last hurricane and said that it was a safe place to wait out the storm."

They lapsed into silence again, listening to the storm outside.

"Are you sure this is a safe place? Maybe we should head further inland."

She couldn't help herself; smiling up at him, she asked, "Where's your sense of adventure?"

He smiled back. "It's standing next to my sense of safety."

Turning back to the fire place, she added, "Don't worry. This is the safest place we could be. We are on one of the tallest peaks. It might get a little windy and we may lose some shingles, but we won't drown and the only flying debris we'll have to worry about are the trees nearby, and Inma told me that after the last hurricane, she had most of the ocean-facing trees removed as a precaution."

Listening again to the growing storm, he decided that there wasn't much more they could do and asked, "Is there anything I can do?"

Anne looked around a moment before answering, "If you wouldn't mind, bring over a couple of lanterns, and then turn off the lights. I'm not sure how long the generator's going to hold out and I'd like to save it for the refrigerator."

James nodded and went to get two lanterns, and then turned off the lights. "Do you have any flashlights?" he asked. "Just in case we need them?"

Anne nodded toward the kitchen. "Top left-hand drawer. You'll find two heavy-duty ones. I put new batteries in them already, and there are spare batteries, just in case," she added as an explanation.

James grabbed the flashlights from the kitchen, putting one in the center of the round kitchen table, and brought the other to the fireplace, setting it on the stone mantelpiece.

Anne stared into the fire. "We should have plenty of firewood, and I've brought enough food and water to last a couple of weeks. Unless all hell breaks loose, we should be fine." Then she smiled at him again, adding, "But I've planned for that as well."

"You're very thorough, aren't you?" He smiled back. "You were a boy scout in another life, weren't you?" She laughed.

Standing, she excused herself and went into the bedroom.

Standing at the large bay window that faced the ocean, she wrestled with her thoughts. She had told him that she wouldn't talk to him tonight, and he had accepted her decision, but now she wasn't sure that she wanted to wait. She wasn't sure that she wanted to hold off the inevitable. Glancing at her watch, she saw that it was just going on 8:00 p.m.; too early to go to bed.

Walking back into the kitchen, she grabbed two glasses and the bottle of Glenlivet and joined James on the sofa again. Her resolution not to drink put aside, she poured two healthy glasses and, setting the bottle on the table, she handed a glass to James. Clinking his glass with hers, she added, "The truth finds a way." Then she took a drink of the scotch.

James watched her. He recognized the quote and realized that the article must have been the catalyst that had prompted her to call him all those months ago. He was about to ask her about that, when she began to talk.

"This isn't going to be easy for me," she began, "I've practiced not talking about myself for so long, I'm not even sure I'll know how to. But in some ways, it will be good to talk about it."

She took another drink for courage and began.

*****

"I think you know most of this already," she began.

"Maybe, but I'd still like to hear it from you," he replied.

"When I was at the police station giving my testimony, I saw someone, a man, whom I had seen before, and I knew I was in trouble."

James wanted to ask her more but decided it would be best to wait until she had told her story. He knew this wasn't easy for her and he didn't want to upset her.

"So, I left the station and I had to run to catch the next train. I just barely caught it. The train was fairly crowded and I was forced to stand. When I got on, I had planned to call my sister, but I got an uneasy feeling; a kind of prickly feeling, like the kind one gets when someone is being watching.

"Looking around, I tried to figure out who was watching me, but I didn't see anyone I recognized. I think I was just feeling paranoid. I got off at my regular stop and went home. I couldn't get my mind off what I had seen and the feeling like I was being followed on the train and I kind of figured that it might be best to go over to my sister's house until I could figure it all out.

"It took me about half an hour to pack some of my things into my backpack and then I realized that going to my sister's wouldn't be the best idea. It probably would be the first place someone would look for me. I called her and told her what had happened."

"What *had* happened?" James prompted her.

Anna took another long drink. "I found something I wasn't supposed to," she admitted. "I had been working for Stephen for over three years, and I would never have thought he would be capable of something like this before…"

"Stephen?" he questioned her.

"My boss…" She frowned, a bit perplexed, before continuing, "Anyway, I had forgotten to print out my boarding pass for a trip I was to go on, and used his laptop. That's when I found the files. I made a quick copy of what I found and then left the office. I was supposed to be going on vacation that night and so I thought I would have time to think about what I should do, but then I realized that I couldn't just let it go, so I went to the police.

"When I got there, I thought I'd be safe. I had given the officer my statement when he had to take a phone call. I got up and went for some coffee. He had showed me where when I first arrived. I was digging in my backpack for some change when I looked up and saw this guy I had seen talking with Stephen in the past. I hid behind a filing cabinet, and then I looked around it to take another look at him. I had to be sure it was him. It was. He was talking to the officer and I suddenly got really scared that I had put myself into more danger, so I walked away. I figured if he had found me at the police station, then I wouldn't be safe anywhere and that I needed to disappear and Chicago suddenly didn't seem large enough for me to hide in so I decided to call my sister and get her help."

"Who was the man you saw at the police station?" he interrupted her.

She frowned at him. "I don't know. I had seen him with Stephen a few times and I never got a good feeling about him."

Then he sat back, a look of surprise evident on his face. "Good god," he whispered. "You're Kiera Davidson."

Pausing, she contemplated lying, but then she nodded. "Yes, I am."

James studied her a moment. Turning his head, he smiled, "You sent me the Douglas USB stick."

She nodded. "I read an article that said you were responsible for disbanding a Chicago gang and thought you'd be the best person to deal with the information on the USB stick." She paused before adding, "I had already told the police the details of what I had seen, but when I saw the guy at the station, I felt sure I wasn't safe. I hadn't told the cops that I had made a copy of everything, so I decided that the FBI should get involved."

She took another drink of the whiskey. "I had already managed to reinvent myself, using my sister's identity, when I read about the senator's murder. I knew I had bigger worries to contend with and decided to really disappear.

"I had been living in Mexico for a few weeks and knew that my, well my sister's, travel visa was about to expire, so I stopped in at the local shop and bought some hair color and got on a bus to Winnipeg, Canada. When I got there, I got off the bus, bought another bus ticket, this time heading to Calgary. There was a two-hour wait, so I took the time to dye my hair and change my clothes.

"When I got to Calgary, I saw a headline that shattered my world. It was the article that said Sari, my sister, had died in a car crash." Swallowing back fresh tears, she continued, "We had agreed not to be in touch, just in case someone was watching her, but when I read the article, I knew that using her passport was no longer an option, so I bought another ticket and headed to Spokane.

"By the time I got to Spokane, I was exhausted. I got a cheap hotel room, bought another bottle of hair dye and some more clothes and spent the next two days sleeping. I kind of settled there for a while. I got a job cleaning people's houses and tried to keep under the radar." She looked up at him.

"I thought I was safe, but then the newspaper ran another article about the senator's murder and I started to feel vulnerable again. Even after I read about the crash and how Sari had been killed, I knew I was still in danger, and despite my feeble attempt to change my appearance, a couple of my clients also saw the resemblance between the two of us and that made me frightened. I couldn't believe Sari had been killed."

Anne closed her eyes to her pain, but carried on, "So, I decided to reinvent myself. A completely new name, a new look. A whole new me. I did a little research on the internet and found the name Charlotte Wood, and decided I'd use it. She had been born in Utah but hadn't ever applied for a social security number. However, on the off-chance that someone knew her, I decided to call myself Cheri Wood, and if anyone noticed the differences, I'd just say that Cheri was a nickname. Once I got the Social, the rest was easy.

"By the time I showed up in Seattle, I had everything set up. But I knew there was always a chance that my past would catch up with me, so I decided I'd create a second identity; that way I'd have everything in place if I ever had to run again. I had decided that if I had to run again, I'd go back to Mexico; this time for good.

"I had met Inma four years before this mess ever started and had always sent her Christmas cards and birthday greetings. So, I started to correspond with her from Seattle, telling her that I was an old college friend of Kiera's and that my name was Anne Manson and that someday I wanted to move to Mexico and that Kiera had suggested I contact her for advice.

"My birth name is Kiera Ann, and my father had always called me Kierann. It was his nickname for me, so it was an easy transition. Manson was my mother's maiden name. Setting up this identity proved to be more challenging, but I eventually got lucky and found someone named Annette Mannson and used her identity to get a passport. I knew that I would be living in Mexico so I wouldn't need a social security number for job purposes, so it was easier."

Looking up at the FBI agent in front of her, she frowned. "I realize I've broken all kinds of fraud and anti-trust laws, but since I was running for my life, I kind of figured it would be seen as a necessary means to an end. Besides, I always thought that once the murderer was convicted, I'd tell the truth and it would all be forgiven. But the article changed that."

Looking down at her hands, she continued, "That's why I called you, to see if the coast was clear. When you told me that it probably wasn't, I knew that I could never be Kiera Davidson again."

Standing up, she went to the fireplace and stoked the embers. "When I got here, Inma told me that she had known all along whom I really was and had kept it to herself for my safety. Only she and her attorney know my true identity."

"And now me," he replied.

"And now you," she admitted. Standing, she returned to her seat and, picking up her glass, took a long drink of the scotch.

*****

She stared into her drink. She felt drained. She had kept the truth a secret for so long. It felt odd having it all out in the open. She hadn't told him everything, only the parts she thought he needed to know. The consequences of telling this handsome FBI agent the truth was still unknown; she only hoped that she hadn't committed any serious crimes that would land her in jail.

Taking a deep breath, she asked the question she dreaded asking. "So, what happens now?"

"I'm not sure," he answered honestly. "I'd like to try and convince you to come back and testify against Douglas, but now…" he shook his head, "I really don't know."

Anne turned toward him. "I'm not going back. I have a new life here now. My sister's gone now," James frowned, and was about to interrupt her when she added, "and Inma is counting on me to run the B&B. My life is here now. Even if this hurricane flattens it to the ground, I'm not going to go back. I'm through looking over my shoulder."

James reached up and touched her hair. Despite all the dyes and bleaching, it was surprisingly soft. He wondered when her sister had died and wanted to console her. Damn it, he hadn't counted on any of this, and he was struggling to come to terms with everything. He knew that he was still attracted to her; perhaps even more so now that he realized just how resourceful she had been to survive. But she was vulnerable right now. He knew that it had taken a lot of courage to expose herself to him like that, and he would not take advantage of that. He would have time to ask her about her family later. Right now, he needed to concentrate on keeping this lovely lady safe.

Anne stood and walked over to the window. The storm had picked up and the rain was driving against the house, which shuddered against it.

She was glad she had told him the truth. Now that everything was out in the open. Whatever happened between them now would be honest.

She had dropped her purse on the chair beneath the window, and she reached into it and took out the photo she kept with her. Studying it again, she smiled at the memory of that day.

Walking back to James, she handed it to him. "I have fond memories of that day," she said as he looked at the photo of the two of them in front of the Seattle Goblin.

James smiled too. He had always wondered what had happened to the disposable camera.

"I have the other photos you took too, if you want them."

James nodded absently, still looking at the photo.

She wondered what he was thinking. Did he think it creepy that she had the photo? By the smile on his lips, she thought not. Perhaps he understood that she had needed some kind of concrete evidence of who she was, or at least of who she had become for the time she had lived in Seattle.

The house shuddered again, and they both looked up toward the ceiling, as if to verify that it was still there.

"We probably should put together an emergency kit, just in case this place doesn't hold up."

Anne smiled at his suggestion. "Already done," she assured him. Then she nodded toward the duffel bag that was leaning against the wall. "We just need to add some clothes for you."

"Are you sure you weren't you a boy scout in a previous life?" he asked in wonderment.

Anne laughed. "No, I just believe in being prepared. There are two sleeping bags, a small tent, matches, flashlights and enough food and water to sustain us for about three days. I figured if the house did collapse, I'd need to hike out or if disaster struck, and I was injured, it would take them about that long to get to me."

As the house shuddered again, she added, "But let's hope that isn't the case. I'd hate to see Inma's retirement home reduced to rubble."

Squatting down in front of the fireplace and stoking the fire, she asked if he would like some more scotch. He shook his head no, and she took the empty glasses and the bottle back into the kitchen. The hum of the refrigerator told her that the generator was still working, and she was thankful for that. Returning to the fire, she stared into the flames.

"I'm glad you're here, James," she admitted.

"So am I." As the storm seemed to pick up a bit, he added, "It's getting late. We should probably try and catch some shut-eye just in case anything does happen."

She nodded in agreement.

*****

The crash woke them both. Anne was out of her bed and running into the hallway in a flash, where she ran into James. Literally. "What was that?" she asked.

"I don't know," he replied.

Anne switched on her flashlight and she saw something in James' hand. Aiming her flashlight down, she saw that he was carrying his gun.

Glancing up at him, she got her answer. "Occupational habit," he explained, then added, "Stay behind me."

They slowly made their way through the cabin, but didn't have long to look for the cause of the noise. The front door had been forced open by a fallen tree. "I think you can put your gun away now," she teased.

"I'm not sure," he teased back. "Didn't you see the Wizard of Oz? We could be in the enchanted forest."

"Could be, but I'd say this one's had it." Turning back toward the bedroom, she said, "Either way, we'd better see if we can get it out of the doorway. I'll get dressed," she added as she closed her bedroom door behind her.

Throwing on a pair of jeans and a sweatshirt, she slipped into her sneakers and once again met James in the hallway. Nodding toward the kitchen, she said, "There are a couple of saws and an axe under the sink"; which got her a questioning look from James. Smiling sneakily, she said, "Best place to keep them between bodies."

"Ha-ha," he said as he went to retrieve the tools. Meanwhile, Anne grabbed a couple of large raincoats and two pairs of work gloves, and then they got to work dismantling the large tree.

Three hours later, they had a nice stack of logs piled next to the fireplace and they were able to close the door again. The rest of the tree would have to wait until they got better equipment.

James helped her clean up the mess left behind and then went to start a small fire in the fireplace while Anne stepped back into the bedroom. Changing out of her dirty clothes, she got back into her striped pajamas and threw on some flannel socks and a flannel shirt for warmth.

Joining James on the sofa, he excused himself to go change and Anne threw another log on the fire. She was glad they had ample stock of dried wood to use. The logs they had just cut wouldn't be ready to burn until they had dried out.

Grabbing a cotton blanket, she snuggled up on the sofa and waited for James' return.

It was nearly four in the morning, and despite feeling exhausted, she knew that she wouldn't get much sleep. The storm had picked up and Anne was sure they were feeling the full brunt of the hurricane. She couldn't help but think of the B&B and she hoped that it wouldn't be totally wiped out. Inma had said that the last hurricane had not done any significant damage, but she had put aside funds and had increased her insurance policy in case she wasn't as lucky the next time.

Her thoughts must have been easy to read, because when James returned, he put his arms around her and in a comforting voice said, "The B&B will be fine. Unless this hurricane ends up worse than expected, I'm sure it will be fine."

Anne smiled up at him. "Thanks, James." Then she turned her head and rested it on his chest. "I really am glad you are here."

He settled them back against the sofa. "Me too." They watched the blazing fire in silence, listening to the storm raging outside.

Anne's eyes began to droop, and she allowed them to close and drifted off to sleep.

James shifted next to her, and she sat up. "Sorry about that," she apologized for drifting off.

James shook his head. "I just thought we'd get a little more comfortable." Stretching his length out on the sofa, he gently pulled her toward him to lay with her back spooned next to him.

While he knew he should insist that she go back to bed, he wasn't ready or willing to let her out of his arms. Not just yet. He knew that he was playing a dangerous game, but he was feeling a little reckless. He had been thinking of holding her in his arms since he first met her, and neither distance, nor the idea that he would never see her again, had diminished the desire.

Anne felt his arm slide around her waist, drawing her closer to him and she felt a sigh escape him. He felt good, she decided, and relaxed against him.

*****

Anne knew that she had been attracted to James since she had first met him, but back in Seattle, she hadn't had the luxury to relax her guard enough to get close to him. In truth, she hadn't felt that she could get close to anyone over the past year and a half, and now that her true identity was out in the open, she felt herself wanting—no, needing to let herself get involved with this man. With James, she wouldn't have to worry about messing up; of saying the wrong thing; of revealing too much of herself. She had kept her true self locked away for far too long and she needed to break free of those bonds.

Turning in his arms, she looked up into his eyes and for the first time in nearly two years, said exactly what she was thinking. "I'm attracted to you," she said bluntly, then smiled and continued, "I've been attracted to you since we first met. But back in Seattle it wasn't safe for me to be attracted to you and so, well, I made sure nothing happened." She could see that he was going to respond, but she laid her finger on his lips to stop him. She wanted to get it all out in the open before he said anything. "James, I haven't allowed myself to be attracted to anyone in quite a while. I'm not saying that I'm desperate or anything like that. In truth I hadn't met anyone until you that I wanted to date. But I wasn't looking to date anyone either. There was too much at stake; too much at risk."

Tilting her head, she searched his eyes for some sign as she added, "But I like you and I am definitely attracted to you. I know that I'm still not completely safe, and that until things change, I'll never be able to be Kiera Davidson again, but well, I guess what I'm trying to say is that I think it's time to get on with my life and stop looking over my shoulder. It's time to let myself date again." She smiled. "I guess what I'm saying is that I'm willing to take the risk if you are."

James studied her face for a moment and then he put all his common sense aside and brought her lips down on his.

*****

It took them two days to get back to the B&B, and to her relief, the damage was minimal. A few broken windows where the boards had been blown off, and some downed trees.

She knew she had been lucky. Other areas of the town had been hit much harder. Her neighbor had a tree fall on their roof, and so she invited them to stay with her until they could get it fixed; however, they had decided to stay with other family members instead, so it was just her and James.

It had taken them the whole day to clean up the mess left by the storm, and it was already getting dark by the time they were able to sit down to relax.

She was wresting with her emotions. Now that he knew her true identity, she wondered what would happen next. What really worried her was that if he had found her, then others might be able to find her as well.

Granted, he had thought she was someone else, but that fact wasn't exactly a comfort, considering the trouble Sari had found herself in. It had cost her her life, and Kiera Anne couldn't help but feel responsible.

*****

James knew that there was only one person he could trust. One person who he could count on to know what to do next.

He picked up his phone and sent a message. He just hoped the man would answer him. He had been out of circulation for over a year, and while it had been reported that he had died, James had always had his doubts, or perhaps he just hoped that was the case. The man had been a good friend and the one man he knew would be able to help them out of this mess.

He would know for sure if his message was answered.

Canada

He hadn't expected the phone call. But the number on the message was one he recognized.

Jumping onto his motorcycle, he drove into town. He knew that she would be at work, and while he didn't want to alarm her, he also knew that they may have to leave quickly.

It had been nearly a year since they had moved to Canada, but they both knew there was always the possibility that they would have to run again.

When he had found her and had learned who she really was, he had instantly realized that he would have to ensure that no one else ever found her again. He had connections that could help them disappear. But first, he had to get them out of the country.

He knew that Connelly would start questioning the delays, and that once he stopped checking in, Connelly would send someone after them, so they had to move fast. They had quickly packed up their belongings, and Sam had done his best to cover up the fact that they had been there.

After he had called Connolly and put his own life on the line, he knew that he had to make sure their tracks weren't traced, so he arranged to have his truck crash into Lake Superior. They had arranged for the truck to be sighted after carefully orchestrating the crash, supporting his claim that she was heading south. He put some distance between himself and the hitman, who was speeding after him, and at the designated area, had slowed slightly to jump out of the car just before it went over the ledge. The car had exploded on impact.

Then he had hidden in the rocks until he saw the hitman arrive at the scene. He had seen him make the call that would ensure their safety. He knew Connelly would want their identity confirmed, so he had contacted a friend in the state medical examiner's office and arranged to have the body of a Jane Doe, fitting Sari's general description, and another that fit his general description, recovered from the wreckage; he had contacted the ME and had arranged to have both their dental records linked to the bodies and confirm that it was indeed them. The bodies were then cremated. He had also arranged to have the word spread that he had been working undercover and had been on the track of a key witness when something had gone wrong and he had died in the crash.

Sam had then hiked back to where he had left Sari, and they had made their way north to the Canadian border. He arranged for an old army buddy to meet them near the border and they chartered a helicopter which took them to Alberta, Canada, where he used his connections to get them a safe place to stay.

Once in Canada, Sam and Sari had remained in hiding for over a month, until Sam was convinced that their ruse had worked. Then, with the help of his connections, Sam arranged for both of them to have new identities. He had explained to Sari that for their own safety, and of their families, they would need to go into witness protection. It would mean they both wouldn't be able to be in touch with their families. Sam had lost his mother when he was a child, and his father had passed away the year before from prostate cancer, leaving Sam with no living family members. He knew it would be harder for Sari, but she seemed to have accepted the conditions he had laid out before her. Sam wasn't sure if she had any other family members, or if she was close to them, but he was relieved when she accepted his terms.

Originally, when they had relocated to Canada, they agreed that it would be best if they keep a distance from each other for a few months. Sari had already learned how to reinvent herself, and they agreed that it would be safest if she kept on her own for a while. If anyone came looking for them, they would have a better chance if they weren't linked.

They would keep in contact through a business contact.

Since Sari had a flare with design, they arranged for her to start a flower shop. As part of the relocation program, Sam arranged to have his life insurance policy sent to a trust fund under the name of a factitious niece, Sara Johnnie. Then he had arranged for Sari to assume the role as his niece, complete with a story that she was his only living relative on his father's side. The story she told people was that she had immigrated to Canada when she was a child with her aunt. The sudden windfall from an uncle she barely knew had come as a surprise.

Now, whenever Sam needed to contact her, he could easily call or stop by the shop to see her, and under the pretense of buying flowers for a friend, he could arrange to meet up with her.

*****

Sari heard the bell on the shop door ring and picked up a towel to wipe the water from her hands. She had been busy prepping some lilies for a wedding arrangement.

Stepping into the showroom, she saw that her assistant was already speaking with one of the ladies from the local church who chose the flowers needed for Sunday mass, and was about to return to the lilies when she saw him. Smiling, she greeted him, "Hello, can I help you with something?"

Sam returned her smile. "Yes, I'd like to have some flowers delivered."

Stepping behind the counter, she started to prepare an order invoice. They had arranged that if Sam needed to meet with her, he would ask to have a box of red roses hand-delivered to the Marriot hotel for an Ann Klein. If it was urgent, then the location would change to the hospital.

"And where will this delivery be to?" she asked hesitantly.

"To the Marriott Hotel. I'd like a box of long-stemmed red roses for Ann Klein."

"Of course; when would you like them delivered?"

"Well, this afternoon if possible."

Sari nodded. Consulting her order book, she saw that she didn't have any new deliveries pending. "Yes, I should be able to arrange for the carrier to deliver them this later this afternoon," she replied, keeping up the ruse.

"Would it be possible to have them delivered earlier? It's kind of a special occasion."

Sari smiled. Glancing down at her schedule again, she nodded. "I think that can be arranged."

Sam paid for the flowers and waved goodbye. He knew that he would see her within the hour. That was the arrangement. Now he had to get over to the Marriott and get a room under the name of Ann Klein.

*****

While it had been their intention to keep their relationship under wraps, over the past year, they had let their guards down and begun seeing each other romantically. They had kept their relationship out of the public eye and would upon occasion use the Ann Klein ruse to have a liaison.

Sari arrived at the hotel room about an hour later. When he opened the door, she stepped into the room and into his arms. "This is an unexpected surprise! I had thought our night together last night would have kept you satisfied." She winked. "Not that I don't mind a midday hook-up now and again." She smiled as she kissed him. Sam deepened the kiss but kept his hands from exploring her curves. While he would love to heat up the sheets with her again, he had to try and keep his mind focused. Sari felt him withdraw from the kiss and knew something was wrong. Sam saw the look of concern creep into her eyes.

Before he could say a word, she asked, "What's wrong? Have they found us?"

Sam led her to the bed and made her sit on it. "I don't know. I got a message today that could mean any number of things. But I wanted you here when I contact him."

"Him?"

"It's someone I used to work with." Seeing the worried look cross her eyes, he added, "Don't worry, he's definitely someone we can trust."

"What could he want?"

Sam shrugged in reply. "But the fact that he sent me a message means that he wants something important."

"Ok, then let's call him," she said bravely.

Sam winked at her. "That's the spirit."

*****

Sam tried the number again. "Third time's the charm," he said as, this time, it was answered. "It's Sam."

Sari watched as Sam listened to what the other person had to say and then he smiled and glanced over at her.

Then Sam spoke to the man on the other line, "Ok, where? Yeah, I think that can be arranged. Give me a couple of days." Hanging up, he smiled. "How would you like to take a trip?"

It Comes Together

72 hours later, they had landed in Acapulco, Mexico. They still weren't out of the woods yet and Sam knew it.

He knew that he was taking a chance bringing her out of hiding. But there was something that Hogan had said that had told Sam that Sari needed to come with him. Maybe, just maybe together, they would be able to close the book on this mess.

Looking over at her, he noticed how tired she looked.

After he had spoken with James Hogan, his old friend, he had once again called on his Canadian contacts and had managed to hitch a ride on a cargo plane, which offered little in the form of comfort. It had been a rough ride.

Sam had long trained himself to be able to sleep in any condition. But Sari hadn't had the same training and from the dark circles under her eyes, it was obvious that she hadn't slept at all.

When they had gotten to Acapulco, Sam had rented a car and they had headed off for the rendezvous point. By his calculations, they would arrive at their destination around midnight.

"You'd better try and get some sleep," he suggested.

"Believe me, I would if I could," she replied in a voice rough with exhaustion. "Actually, is there any chance that we could stop and get a bite to eat? I'm starving," she said as she pointed toward a McDonald's sign.

Sam realized that it was more than sleep they were lacking. "Sure. But it will have to be to-go."

Sari nodded and whispered "Thank you" as he pulled into the McDonald's drive-through lane. While Sam ordered, Sari ran into the fast-food restaurant and used the facilities. They were back on the road within 10 minutes. Twenty minutes later, Sam glanced over and saw that she had finally fallen asleep.

*****

Sari woke with a start. Looking around, she saw that they were still driving, but she had no idea where she was.

The last three days seemed a blur. She vaguely remembered that they had landed in Mexico, but that was all she really knew. Sam hadn't told her much; the fact was that he didn't know much either. But something that had been said to him made him believe that this was important; important enough to risk discovery.

Sam glanced over and noticed that she had awoken. "How do you feel?"

"Still pretty tired," she admitted. "Where are we?"

"Somewhere near Salina Cruz." He handed her the map and pointed at their location.

"Is that where we are to meet him? Salina Cruz?"

Sam nodded. "If all goes well."

Sari frowned at his reply. "Is there a chance he won't be there?"

"He said that he would try," was Sam's reply. "From what I gathered, the hurricane left the roads a little worse for wear, so he might have some problems getting there. We are to wait a few days, and if he doesn't show, he'll give me a call to arrange a different meeting place."

Sari looked out at the countryside around them and finally took notice of a number of downed trees. "I completely forgot about the hurricane. It mainly hit on the western side of the country, didn't it?"

"Yes, it wiped out a number of small fishing villages." He frowned. "It's really going to affect the economic condition of the country." He saw the sign he had been looking for and slowed down to turn right. "Nearly there. We've been booked into a small hotel on the coast."

Sari nodded.

"To avoid any suspicion, we'll be sharing a room. I hope that's ok with you." They hadn't been dating long and he didn't want to make any assumptions.

She smiled. "I think I can trust you."

*****

After they checked into the B&B, Sam contacted James again and arranged to meet the next day at one of the beach houses that had been abandoned during the storm. It would give them the privacy they needed for the first meeting.

Both Sam and James knew that this first meeting could be dangerous if anyone was watching them. James had scouted out the place and felt that it would give them the best cover. Sam decided that it would be best to let Sari stay at the hotel for this first meeting. Just in case anything went wrong.

The next morning, they rose early and after breakfast, he left her sitting by the pool.

*****

It was after noon when James and Anne arrived at the meeting place. She was surprised that the hurricane hadn't really touched this part of the country. The house looked unused, but structurally sound.

Stepping out of the jeep, she walked toward the house. But then she felt her world turn upside down. As she walked in behind James, she came face to face the man she had seen at the police station. The man she thought had been after her all along. She turned and ran.

James caught up to her as she started the jeep. "Anne, what is it? What's wrong?"

Anne wasn't sure what to do. She had thought she could trust him, but he had just led her into a trap.

"Stay away from me, James," she screamed.

"No, I'm not losing you again," he said as he reached for her. "Now, what is this all about? What has got you so spooked?"

Sam had begun to approach them and was watching the exchange.

Anne looked up and saw him and felt the fear take a firm grip inside her. "I thought I could trust you, James, but obviously, I was wrong."

James looked back at Sam and felt even more confused. "Sam is a federal agent," he began to explain.

"He works for Stephen Douglas. He's a murderer," she screamed, "and you set me up," she added as she reached for the gears.

"Damn it, Anne. Stop it." James' anger began to rise as he reached to stop her. "You're not making sense."

It was then that James felt Sam's hand on his shoulder. "Get her into the house."

But something in his voice made James hesitate. "What is it?"

"Just get her into the house, and then I'll explain everything."

Sam couldn't afford to have the woman draw attention to them. Things were precarious as it was without her screaming he was a killer.

James turned back to Anne and noticed that she was trembling. "Anne, I need you to come back into the house."

But she shook her head no. "It's him," she whispered.

"Him, who?"

"The man who works for Stephen. The man who's been chasing me," she whispered as she put the jeep in gear and sped off.

James turned to find Sam staring at him. Then he noticed the gun.

Sam couldn't afford to have his cover blown, and until he had a chance to find out more about what the girl had said to James, he'd have to play it safe.

"Sam, what the hell is this all about?"

"Get in the car," was his reply, as he motioned toward his rental car.

James didn't want to lose Anne, but he wasn't sure what Sam was up to. He realized that the more they delayed, the harder it would be to track her. Maybe if he could get the gun off Sam, he'd have a chance to catch up with her.

Sam could see James hesitate; he could see his mind start to calculate whether or not he could take him. "Just get in the god damn car," he answered the unspoken question.

As James got in, Sam knocked him on the back of the head, rendering him unconscious. Then he got in behind the wheel and sped off in the direction he had seen the girl go.

Within minutes, he had caught up with her, but he kept his distance. He would wait until the time was right to grab her.

He was glad he had left Sari at the hotel; otherwise, he would have had to take care of her as well.

*****

Anne took the corner quicker than she should have and she felt the jeep begin to tip.

Taking her foot off the accelerator, she straightened her tires and felt the vehicle settle back on the pavement. "Don't get yourself killed," she scolded herself.

She had to find a safe place to hide. She didn't know whether James was involved or not, but the fact that he knew the hitman didn't settle well with her.

What the hell was she going to do? She had thought that her troubles were all behind her, but when they had gotten to the meeting place and she had seen the hitman approaching them, she knew her problems were far from over.

"Damn it!" She had trusted James, and he had led her straight to the one person she feared the most.

Pulling up to a stoplight, she closed her eyes to the tears that threatened to spill. She took a deep breath and tried to decide what to do, when a thought came to her.

James had seemed honestly surprised by her leaving. Granted, he had managed to fool her up until now, but why hadn't he just grabbed her and forced her to go with him? No one was around. He could easily have manhandled her.

What if she had been wrong? What if he truly hadn't known that the other man was Stephen's henchman?

Oh god, what if she had put him in danger?

As the light changed to green, she knew she had to turn back. Doing a quick U-turn, she spun the jeep around and headed back toward the abandoned seaside B&B.

Sam caught sight of her and pulled the car over, ducking down behind the wheel until she had passed. Then he turned around and followed her back to the beach. Pulling his car up behind her parked jeep, he got out and pointed the gun at her. "Unless you want your friend hurt, I suggest you come with me."

Anne had to fight the urge to run. Looking into the passenger seat, she saw James slumped in the seat, and her fear was replaced with anger. "What have you done to him?" She demanded.

"He's only knocked out. For now," he added the threat to ensure her compliance.

She understood the veiled threat and stepped up to the car.

Sam stepped back and motioned her into the driver's seat. "You're driving. But don't try anything funny. We both know what I am capable of, and I don't miss—ever."

Anne slid in behind the wheel and looked over at James. "He's fine," Sam said from behind her. "Now drive."

The drive was a short one. Sam had seen the abandoned beach hut about a mile away that would suit his purpose. He needed to find a phone and call Sari. The cellular cover was non-existence on the beach and his cell phone wasn't working. He knew that if he was delayed, Sari would start to worry, and he couldn't afford to have her get spooked and bolt as well.

*****

He left the girl and James tied up in the hut. He would have to deal with them later, but first he needed to get a hold of Sari. They had agreed that if something went wrong and if she hadn't heard from him within an hour, she was to take the money he had left her and leave. She was a resourceful woman and he had no doubt that she would be able to, once again, make a new life for herself.

But now wasn't the time.

He had been driving about 15 minutes when he saw the small town he had passed on his way to the beach where he had met James. He soon spotted a phone booth and pulled up next to it. It looked a little worse for wear, having all the windows busted, and by the smell of it, someone had used it as a toilet, but there was a dial tone and after he entered the coins needed, he was relieved to hear her voice at the other end of the phone.

"Hello?" she answered hesitantly.

"It's Sam. My cell phone isn't working, so I had to find a pay phone," he explained, and he could hear her relax.

"How did it go?"

"Fine," he lied, "but we need to work out some more details before I come pick you up. Ok?"

Sam had told Sari that he was meeting someone who might make it possible for them to come out of hiding, so she knew it was something that could take some delicate planning. "Ok, how long?"

"I'm not sure, it could be a couple of hours. Do you have enough to do?"

Sari laughed. "Oh, I think I could be persuaded to soak up some more rays and sip some more margaritas."

"Good. Then I'll leave you to it and I'll give you a shout as soon as I can."

"Alright," she replied.

Then Sam added, "But Sari, if you don't hear from me by five o'clock, then you know what to do."

"Is there a chance of that?" He could hear worry in her voice.

Forcing a smile on his face and into his voice, he replied, "No, but until I know that everything is set, I want to keep you safe."

167

"I understand." She seemed to relax.

"Sari, everything is going to be ok. I'm just being cautious."

Sam could hear the smile in her voice. "Thank you."

"Now, go enjoy the sun and I'll see you soon."

As he hung up the phone, he hoped he had calmed her fears and that she wasn't suspicious of anything.

Then he headed back to the hut.

*****

Anne tried again to loosen the ropes that were tied around her hands, and thought she felt them give slightly. She didn't think she had much time. She wasn't sure why the hitman had left, but she knew he would be back.

Looking over at James, she tried again to wake him. The man had gagged her, but she was still able to make some noise with her voice and she hoped that it would be loud enough to wake him. The hitman had also bound him, but hadn't gagged him, so she hoped that if he would wake up, then he may be able to yell for help.

Looking around the hut, she noticed the place look largely unused. There were a few empty cans of beer in the corner, and she wonder if perhaps this was a hangout for the local kids. Maybe, if they were lucky, some of the kids would decide to come by the hut.

Anne was trying to loosen her gag again when she heard a car drive up. She hoped her efforts wouldn't be noticed by her abductor.

But when Sam entered the hut, she knew that he could instantly see that she had been struggling against the ropes, trying to loosen them.

Glancing over at James, he saw that he was unconscious. Setting the bag of supplies he had picked up on the old wooden table, he walked up next to Anne. Crouching down, he pulled the gag off her mouth. "You can scream if you want, but no one will hear you."

Hearing a voice, James started to rouse from his state of unconsciousness.

Anne looked over at James, and was about to speak when the man in front of her rose and went to him. "How's the head?" he asked James.

James forced his eyes open and looked at Sam. "What the hell happened?"

Sam shrugged. "It couldn't be avoided," was his answer.

As Sam stepped back, James studied Anne. "Are you ok?" he asked.

Anne nodded, not trusting her voice and not wanting to lose control over her emotions.

James let the venom of his anger spill over. "Sam, what the hell is this all about?"

Instead of replying, Sam walked up to the table and started to take several items out of the bag.

James waited. When he had first confirmed that Sam was indeed still alive, he had been relieved and hadn't thought twice about bringing him into his confidence. He hadn't questioned why Sam had faked his own death, but now, as he watched Sam place several bottles of water, bandages and other obscure items on the table, he wondered if perhaps he had been wrong about Sam's character.

Then Sam turned and asked, "Who else did you talk to about our little meeting?"

James frowned. "No one, unfortunately," he admitted.

Then Sam turned toward the girl and repeated the question.

"Who would I have told?" she answered in defeat.

Sam thought for a moment and then turned back to address James. "What do you know about Senator Millstone's case?"

"You mean murder," Anne spat out.

Sam ignored her outburst and continued to study James.

"Only the information that was left in the file," was his reply. "An eyewitness claimed to see the murder from the building across the way. She supposedly got photos of the event, which went missing, and then she went missing as well."

"Anything else?" Sam continued to study James.

James frowned. He could tell that Sam was looking for something, but he didn't have a clue of what that might be. He thought about the entire case, not only what was in the file. Despite the circumstances, he confirmed the other point that made up the bulk of his case. "Douglas's legal assistant went missing a month before. It was thought that she had information that would prove he was trying to blackmail Millstone."

"Go on," Sam prompted him.

James wanted to protect Anne's true identity as long as possible. "Ok, it was more than just a thought. The woman had sent the file to my desk, which partially led to his conviction." Sam continued to wait. James studied the man he had thought was his friend. What was he waiting for?

Closing his eyes, he tried to remember everything he had read about the case. There had been the evidence from the scene, the forensics and, of course, the medical examiner's report. Opening his eyes, he stared at Sam as he realized what had been missing. How he had missed it before, he wasn't sure, but it was so blatant now.

"The ME's report," he acknowledged.

Sam waited for James to start connecting the dots. He needed him to connect the dots and to come up with the right answers. If he didn't, then Sam would be forced to act accordingly, and he didn't relish the idea of harming his old friend.

James looked over at Anne who looked obviously confused. He didn't want to say anything that would put her in danger, but he needed to verify his suspicions. He realized that the ME's report hadn't been signed. It may have been an oversight, but he doubted it, which meant that there was a lot more going on than a witness running scared.

Now was the tricky part, he needed to confirm his suspicions without endangering Anne's position, and he thought he knew how.

"Does Shep know?" He quizzed him.

Sam didn't blink, which told him that even Shep was in the dark about this one. "Well, I suppose you couldn't risk bringing him in on it. He's a good man, but he would want to keep his reputation intact."

Sam finally gave him an indication that he was on the right track. "That's a fact."

Squatting down in front of James, Sam started to untie his bindings. "Sorry about the head," he said, "but I had to be sure."

Anne looked from one man to the next and tried to figure out what was going on.

When he was untied, James went to Anne and started to untie the ropes that held her. She was shaking. "Everything is going to be alright," he tried to reassure her. Pulling her to her feet, he steered toward the table and had her sit down, and then he turned to Sam. He was angry that he had been kept in the dark for so long. "I think it's time you bring us up to speed."

Sam nodded. "I have to admit that I had no idea that the 'witness' you mentioned on the phone was this witness," he said as he nodded toward Anne. "Miss Davidson, I'm sorry for scaring you."

Anne looked up at James. "I don't understand."

Sam was the one to answer her question. "What I am about to tell you is highly classified. Part of me isn't even sure that you should hear it but considering your… how should I say…unique position in this matter, I think you should."

Then Sam sat down at the table across from her. "Let me begin by saying that I am not a murderer. What Sari saw was staged. No one but a select number of people were supposed to see it happen. In many ways, her witnessing it helped seal the deal."

Anne shook her head. "I don't understand."

Sam nodded. "Sari saw what she was supposed to see. More specifically, what Stephen Douglas was supposed to see."

"But how did you—" She still wasn't convinced.

"The report stated that the witness who saw the senator shot several times," James cut in. "That was what Douglas was supposed to see. But what he couldn't have known was that the senator was very much alive."

"The police…" She shook her head.

"A staged event," James said beneath his breath.

"A staged event?" Anne looked up at him.

James nodded. "A staged event. Hire an actor who looked like, or should I say, was made to look like the victim, and then simulate death," James answered her.

"Simulate death," she repeated.

Sam nodded. "Actually, the senator was happy to play the part himself. Add in your own special team of paramedics and a ME who is on your side, and it's easy to help someone disappear."

"Disappear?" Anne shook her head in denial.

"Douglas saw exactly what he was supposed to see. I must admit, it took some work to convince the senator to agree to it, but once we explained that being caught *in flagrante* with several underaged males and that losing his political seat and a reduced prison sentence for his cooperation was far less dangerous than succumbing to the blackmail attempt, he was on board. We had suggested using a body double, but he was afraid Douglas would see through the disguise, so he agreed to act the part. We knew that Douglas had someone on the force, so we couldn't risk pulling in the local PD, so I was brought in to accept the hit and we brought in our own team to assist."

"But what about the phone call?" James asked, remembering Sari's testimony of what she had witnessed at the shooting.

"That was Douglas confirming that Millstone was dead. Of course, we hadn't expected our witness to see everything." He looked over toward Anne. "When you disappeared, we thought you were another one of Connelly's victims, so this was our only shot at getting him indicted. We had arranged for evidence to be found at the scene that would be linked to Connelly. But the scene got compromised. We just got lucky when the witness made the call. We certainly hadn't expected the police to be called in so quickly, but… well, in some ways, it worked out for the best. When the local guys got to the scene quicker than expected, and then the photos went missing, it confirmed our suspicions that the chief was on the take. He was the only other person, aside from the investigating officers, who had access to the evidence."

"But how did you know it was him and not the other officers?" Anne asked.

"We didn't at first, but I knew that Shep wasn't involved—"

"Shep? Is that Detective Shep Wilson?" she asked.

Sam nodded. "Yes, he's my brother-in-law, and when his partner was killed—"

"Detective Kollar was killed?" she whispered.

"Yes," he confirmed.

"How?" she asked.

"After he read about the witness' death in the car crash, he went to Northern Minnesota to find you, but the cabin he was staying in had a suspicious gas leak which leveled the building."

James frowned. "I read about that. Didn't the cabin belong to their chief?"

Sam nodded. "Initially, it was thought it was just a gas leak. The chief had told the investigating team that he had been having problems with it, and had told Kollar not to use the stove. But upon further investigation, it was determined that someone had sabotaged the valve on the gas tank and had left a long fuse. Despite the condition of his body, the autopsy confirmed that he had been shot first, and then the valve had been tampered with."

She sat there in shock. "The senator's alive," she whispered in disbelief.

"Officially, the senator was murdered," Sam said in response.

Anne stood up and walked to the window. Her mind was racing. The 'hitman' had actually turned out to be a cop. She asked, "What happens now?"

Sam glanced at his watch and addressed James. "I've got to make a few phone calls. I'll drop you off at your jeep and I'd like to meet you in a couple of hours. There's someone I think you should meet, and then we'll figure out what to do next."

James looked puzzled, but decided that he would trust Sam.

*****

Sari rolled over onto her back and set her book down. Closing her eyes, she was trying to decide if she should put on more suntan lotion or if she would be ok, when a shadow passed over her.

Opening her eyes, she looked up and smiled. "Hello stranger."

Sam sat down on her chair next to her and smiled. "Hello to you. You're already getting quite the tan."

"Finally." She laughed. "I feel like I haven't gotten a proper tan in years." Sitting up, she asked, "What time is it?"

"Nearly 3:30," he said as he took a sip of her margarita.

"How did your meeting go?"

"Very well," Sam decided. "In fact, if you don't mind, I'd like you to meet someone."

"Your friend?"

Sam didn't answer that; instead, he said, "It'll mean that we need to get moving."

"Ok," she replied and began to gather her things together.

*****

Within the hour, Sari was showered, dressed and packed. Sam checked them out of the B&B, explaining that they had been called back to the States on urgent business, and then they headed toward the airport.

At the airport, Sam returned the rental car and then they took a taxi to another B&B. Sam and Sari arrived at the B&B at the predetermined time James and he had arranged and went to the room that had been reserved.

Knocking on the door, James opened it and motioned Sam in. Sari followed Sam into the room and stopped in her tracks. Standing there in front of her was someone who looked so much like her, she had to smile.

James held out his hand. "Hello, I'm James Hogan. You must be Sari Manning. It's a pleasure to meet you."

Sari shook his hand but continued to look at the woman before her. James continued, "Allow me to introduce you to Anne Manson; formerly, Kiera Davidson."

Anne stepped around James and rushed to hug the woman before her. "You're still alive."

Sari couldn't stop the smile that formed. "I guess I could say the same thing to you."

Sam frowned down at Sari. "You know each other?"

Anne laughed. "This is my sister. Sari."

"Well, half-sister," Sari smiled up at him, "but we've always been so close that we've dropped the half part."

Sam shook his head. "I think you better explain."

Kiera Anne spoke up, "Our dad wasn't what you'd call a conventional guy. He was seeing both our mothers in college and they both got pregnant about the same time. Sari is two months older than me. I guess some people would call us Irish twins. We've also looked so alike that we were often mistaken for actual twins whenever Dad had both of us.

"Anyway, Sari's mom wasn't happy with Dad's infidelity, and the constant reminder that we looked so alike really bothered her, so she moved them to Minnesota."

Sari nodded and continued the story, "Dad died when we were in high school, and we got back in touch and kept in touch. When my mom passed away from cancer a few years ago, I decided to move back to Chicago. I got a job opportunity and we started to hang out more."

Turning toward Anne, she continued, "When Kiera called me and told me about what she had seen in her boss's office, and how she thought she had been found out, we decided that she should become me. We were both supposed to take a trip to Mexico, and well, for obvious reasons, it didn't seem possible for her to go—at least not under her passport and boarding pass, so I gave her my documents and my ID and she went to Mexico as me. As Sari Manning. Kiera always called me Siri. Like the Apple assistant. It's our own private joke. Who do you ask for help? You ask Siri." She smiled at her sister. "We figured no one would realize the connection. Then I laid low, driving up to Wisconsin and staying in a cabin a friend of mine owns.

"I didn't tell my boss about the change of plans because I thought the less people who knew about the switch, the better. I knew that my friend was visiting family in Maine, so I borrowed her cabin for a couple of weeks. Then when I was supposed to return from Mexico, I threw on some spray tan and told everyone I had a great time."

"Meanwhile," Kiera Anne picked up the story, "I hung out in Mexico until I read about the senator's murder. I've been estranged from my mom for a while, so I didn't have to worry about keeping her in the loop. At first, they hadn't mentioned Sari's name as the witness, so I didn't know she had been pulled into my same nightmare, until I read about the car crash."

Reaching down, she grabbed her sister's hand, "I thought you had died in that car crash."

Sari gave her a hug. "I know. I wanted to tell you, but I was so afraid I'd get found out and I couldn't jeopardize your safety. As far as I knew, you were still listed as missing and I couldn't risk it."

Sam had been studying the two women and he shook his head. "You are definitely sisters."

"…and uncannily alike," James added.

Sam laughed. "You can say that again. Despite everything, you both managed to become involved in the same crime, and you both managed to disappear and successfully reinvent yourselves."

James motioned to Sam and they left the women on their own to catch each other up on what had been happening in their lives.

Stepping out on the balcony, James turned to Sam. "Sam, I had called you because I needed your help. If I found Anne, I mean Kiera, then we both know that Connelly's henchmen are bound to find her as well."

Nodding, Sam agreed, "I think you're right."

James leaned against the balcony. "I had hoped that when I got Douglas, if, by some miracle, either of these ladies were still alive, they would be safe. But then Connelly came into the picture and I figured that if either of them had been alive, he would have found them and made sure that they would never be able to testify." James looked back at Sam. "When I heard about your death, my first thought was that the bastards had won."

Then James grinned. "But then I got some information, a tape, actually. It was a recording of Connelly hiring a certain hitman to find Sari and make sure she was dead. That was all the proof I needed to convict the man."

Sam winked. Then he sobered. "So, what are we going to do now?"

"That's a good question. Douglas and Connelly may both be behind bars, but I still can't guarantee that they wouldn't use their influence to get to these ladies." James looked over at the women, who were now huddled in conversation.

"Their testimonies need to be recorded, if for no other reason than to guarantee that those sons of bitches, Douglas and Connelly, never get out of prison. But the question is how to do that without putting them in harm's way?"

Sam agreed. "I have an idea. I need to make a few phone calls, but I think there's really only one thing we can do."

Vancouver Gazette

Police investigating a suspicious death.

The charred remains of two individuals, a man and a woman, were discovered in a burned-out cabin in Vancouver, Canada.

Dental records have identified the remains to be that of FBI Agent James Hogan and Kiera Davidson. Agent Hogan had last been seen in the Seattle area where he had been investigating the disappearance of Miss Cheri Wood. Miss Wood disappeared under mysterious circumstances after being threatened by Connelly's men.

A statement issued by the director of the FBI: "We have reason to believe that during his investigation, Agent Hogan had made some connections behind the disappearance of Ms. Wood and that of Kiera Davidson, the assistant to convicted murderer, Stephen Douglas, who had gone missing shortly before his conviction. Agent Hogan was last reported following a lead to Ms. Davidson's location in Canada when he was killed. Ms. Davidson, previously believed to be one of five missing persons, disappeared after being threatened by known hitmen, who have been convicted of murder for hire by crime boss Joe Connelly.

"Ms. Woods' location is still unknown, but it is believed that she has joined the list of missing persons associated with Connelly.

"In a related investigation, the FBI have uncovered previously missing testimony from two of the key witnesses that identify both Douglas and Connelly as the masterminds behind Senator Millstone's murder. The taped interviews with the two witnesses had been missing from the evidence file at the time of the highly publicized court cases."

Sources close to the FBI have confirmed that Chief John Harris has been directly linked to the missing testimonies and is currently under investigation, along with several other members of the Chicago police force under allegations of tampering with evidence and witness intimidation.

Furthermore, Chief Harris is being investigated as a possible suspect in the murder of Detective Jason Kollar who lost his life when the cabin he was staying in exploded. The cabin had been owned by the chief at the time of the explosion.

Police are following several lines of inquiry, and ask for individuals to come forward if they have any information regarding these investigations.

The End

Epilogue

James snuck up behind her and grabbed her by the waist. Sari jumped and dropped the brochures that were in her hands. Turning, she narrowed her eyes at him. "Wrong sister, you nincompoop." Then she smiled.

They found it funny that the guys got them mixed up. The fact that they both enjoyed wearing similar clothes and had the same hairstyle was often the cause of the mix-up. They still found it humorous. "Your wife is in one of the bedrooms making the bed for the next guest." James had the grace to blush before heading up to find his wife.

Bending to pick up the tourist brochures, she heard Sam chuckling. Looking up, she shook her head. "Don't even pretend that you haven't done that as well."

Sam squatted down in front of his wife and helped her gather the slips of paper. "That's true, sweetheart, but one look at you from the front, and anyone could see the difference."

Sari smiled up at him as he helped her to her feet and then laid her hand against her thickening waist. "Maybe," she conceded. But she knew that it wouldn't be for long. Kiera had confided in her earlier this morning that she was expecting a child of her own, and from the shout of joy that suddenly came from upstairs, she knew Kiera had just told her husband the good news.

www.ingramcontent.com/pod-product-compliance
Lightning Source LLC
Chambersburg PA
CBHW051112050726
47592CB00002B/785